THE RED SPECTACLES GANG

'What's *your* name?' asked Caroline.

'Ricky. Ricky Redman.'

Kenneth gave a wink and a nod to Caroline.

'What's up?' Ricky asked.

'Oh . . . nothing, really,' said Kenneth. 'It's just that we heard you left your last school . . . involuntarily.'

'I was expelled, if that's what you mean.'

'Tough luck,' said Fen.

'Not really.' Ricky smiled. 'I didn't like the place.'

'I doubt if you'll find Spencer's much of an improvement,' said Fen with a laugh.

'It all depends whether he wants to fit in or not,' said Kenneth, 'and I certainly don't think those clothes fit in with Spencer's standards!'

The Red Spectacles Gang

Gordon Snell

RED FOX

A Red Fox Book
Published by Random House Children's Books
20 Vauxhall Bridge Road, London SW1V 2SA

A division of Random House UK Ltd

London Melbourne Sydney Auckland
Johannesburg and agencies throughout the world

First published by Hutchinson Children's Books 1991

Red Fox edition 1992

Text © Gordon Snell 1991

Printed and bound in Great Britain by
Cox & Wyman Ltd, Reading, Berkshire

ISBN 0 09 989480 7

For dearest Maeve, with all my love

1

'What's that smell coming from your satchel, Edward?'

The tall, fair-haired boy was staring at the smaller one, smiling. But the smile was not friendly.

'There isn't any smell!' said Edward.

'No smell?' Kenneth, the tall boy, asked. He held his nose and looked at the girl and boy beside him.

'No smell?' they echoed, holding their noses too. They were grouped round Edward, who was standing with his back to the playground wall, just inside the tall brick pillars of the entrance gate.

The playground was crowded as the blue-uniformed pupils of Spencer's School waited for the signal to go inside. One of the rules at Spencer's – and there were a lot of rules – was that everyone had to wait for the shrill sound of the bell before lining up ready to go in to the school for the morning assembly.

Even in winter, or when it was pouring with rain, they still had to wait outside. The headmaster, Mr Maddox, told them this was all part of the discipline and character-building which made Spencer's the great school it was.

'What do you think the smell is, Simon?' asked Kenneth.

'Perhaps it's Edward,' said Simon.

'Yes, perhaps it's Edward,' said the girl, Caroline.

'Or perhaps it's Edward's lunch,' said Kenneth,

suddenly snatching the satchel. Kenneth was a school prefect, and liked bullying people and bossing them around.

'Give it back!' shouted Edward. He wished once again that his parents would let him have the school lunch. But every time he asked them about it they started arguing with each other, which they did all the time about everything. So Edward had stopped asking. He just put up with the rather dull cheese sandwich his mother made every day.

Now Kenneth was holding the satchel up in the air, making Edward reach for it. But he couldn't get to it, especially as the heavy bulk of Simon was between him and Kenneth.

'Here, Caroline, catch!' said Kenneth, throwing the satchel to her. She caught it, and just as Edward tried to snatch it from her, she threw it to Simon, who passed it back to Kenneth.

Kenneth put his hand into it, took out the paper bag with the sandwich in it, and dropped it on the ground.

'Oh dear,' he said, 'look what's fallen out! You can have your satchel back, Edward – I think we've found what's causing the stink.'

Edward gripped the satchel and could only stare gloomily as Kenneth picked up the paper bag and took out the thick white slabs of bread.

'Yuk!' he said, holding the sandwich away from him. 'I don't know why you can't have a school lunch like any decent person, instead of bringing this sort of disgusting object to school.'

'It's not disgusting,' said Edward.

'Oh, don't you think so?' said Kenneth. 'Then you might as well have it back. Catch!' He deliberately threw the sandwich to the left of Edward, who jumped to try and catch it, but missed. The sandwich fell on to the ground.

'Oh, what a shame,' said Kenneth. 'You'll never make a rugby player if you can't catch better than that.'

'Maybe he doesn't want to be a rugby player.' The voice came from a dark-haired girl wearing a bright blue shirt. Her name was Fenella, but she didn't like that, so she called herself Fen, much to her mother's annoyance.

'Who asked *you*?' said Kenneth.

'Yes, who asked *you*?' echoed Caroline.

'Don't worry, Fen,' said Edward quietly as he bent to pick up the sandwich.

'He's no right to bully you like that.'

'Bully? Me?' said Kenneth in mock surprise.

'I'll give you some of *my* lunch, Edward,' said a black-haired boy, coming over to the group. 'My mother always packs a lot.'

'Thanks, Stass,' said Edward. Stass's full name was Anastasios, but even he agreed that it was a bit of a mouthful to say.

'I'm sure he'd rather eat that grubby sandwich than the Greek muck your lot eat,' said Kenneth.

Stass didn't reply. He simply put his head down and ran like a bull at Kenneth, butting him in the stomach. Kenneth gave a gasp, then leaped at Stass and grabbed his neck in an arm lock.

'What a nerve, attacking a prefect,' said Kenneth.

'What a nerve!' shrieked Caroline gleefully, and aimed a kick at Stass's legs.

'Get off him!' said Fen, pulling Caroline away.

'Leave her alone!' said Simon, grabbing Fen's arm. Edward jumped on to Simon's back, and they

3

both fell to the ground, Simon dragging Fen and Caroline with him.

'STOP THIS AT ONCE, ALL OF YOU!'

They all froze into stillness, gazing up from their tangled heap on the ground. Above them loomed the grim figure of Mrs Froom, the deputy head. She had shiny grey hair, short and carefully shaped, so that it looked as if she was wearing a helmet. Her eyes were grey too, and seemed to have a piercing quality, as though she was pointing two laser beams at you.

Kenneth released Stass, and said: 'He just rushed at me, Mrs Froom. I don't know why.'

'Well, Anastasios, explain yourself.' Mrs Froom's voice was harsh and rasping, like sandpaper scraping on wood.

'He insulted me,' said Stass.

'Did you, Kenneth?'

'Oh no, Mrs Froom,' said Kenneth, with pretended innocence.

'Not much! You big-headed slob!' said Fen.

'That will be enough of that!' snapped Mrs Froom. 'Anastasios! Fenella! You will stay in after school and do two hours' detention. The locker rooms need a good clean-out.'

'But that's not fair!' said Edward.

'Any more whining from you, boy, and you'll be joining them.' Mrs Froom's laser eyes glared at Edward. Kenneth and his friends were looking on with smug smiles on their faces.

Edward gulped, and said: 'It really wasn't their fault, Mrs Froom. Kenneth grabbed my satchel—'

'YOU DARE TO ANSWER ME BACK?' Mrs Froom's voice was like a whip cracking. 'You're in the locker room after school, too. Unless you'd prefer me to take you along to the headmaster? I'm sure he could find an even more unpleasant job for you.'

Edward shook his head glumly. The headmaster did indeed have a knack of thinking up unpleasant punishments, like cleaning the lavatories or polishing up all the saucepans in the domestic science room. Once he had even got two people to sweep the front steps of the school, using toothbrushes.

Mr Maddox believed in discipline for its own sake. If a punishment was unfair, you shouldn't complain, you should just 'take it on the chin', as he liked to say. He said it was whining and complaining against authority that was undermining the fabric of the nation. Spencer's must be a torch that would light up the old values and traditions that had made the country great.

Fen and Stass admired Edward for standing up for them, but they knew now it was useless to try to get any justice against Kenneth. He managed to make himself a teacher's pet to the staff, while bullying as much as he could when there was no one to find him out.

The sound of the bell sliced through the air. It was so piercing and shrill that it made you jump, even when you heard it several times a day. Mr Maddox had decided that the best way to attract attention was to use the fire-alarm system instead of an ordinary bell. No one dared to ask him how he would go about signalling an actual fire.

Mrs Froom beamed one final glare at Edward, then strode across the playground towards the main entrance of the school. At the top of the steps, Mr Grimley, the caretaker, was just opening the big double doors wide. He was an elderly man, who always wore a brown coat and a carpenter's apron, the pockets often heavy with tools, or boxes of screws and nails. He had thick glasses and peered about as he moved along with his stooped, shuffling step.

The teaching staff, and Mrs Froom especially, treated him with scorn. Today he could be seen greeting her as she marched up the steps, but she swept past him without even glancing at him.

'Line up! Line up!' The prefects were getting the classes into lines. Kenneth was enjoying giving orders, as usual. He was in Class 5A, one of the two classes in the school which had the oldest pupils. Kenneth boasted that after Spencer's he was going on to a top public school, where his father and all his family had gone.

Mr Maddox knew Kenneth's father, who had given a lot of money to the school for various projects, so the headmaster always treated Kenneth well and overlooked anything he did wrong. The most recent project Mr Johnson had contributed hugely to was the swimming pool which had been built near the pavilion at the edge of the playing field.

It was a good pool, but always ice-cold because Mr Maddox thought cold water was good for the character and refused to have any heating installed. What was more, he insisted that each class go swimming once a week at least, even on wet days. And they weren't allowed to splash about and enjoy themselves: everyone had to swim six lengths of the pool, without stopping.

As the classes formed up in the playground, Kenneth was gazing at the three lines of Class 5A like a general inspecting his troops.

He said to Fenella: 'Is that shirt supposed to be school uniform?'

'It's blue, isn't it?' said Fen, looking down admiringly at her shiny shirt, silky and bright.

'Day-Glo blue, I'd call it,' Kenneth sneered. Simon gave a snort of laughter, and Caroline giggled.

'Well, I saw Mrs Froom staring at it,' Kenneth went on, 'and we'll soon see if the headmaster thinks it's correct school uniform. Don't say I didn't warn you.'

'Thank you, Kenny,' said Fen, who knew he hated being called that. Kenneth glowered at her. Just then a loud referee's whistle sounded.

Mrs Froom was standing at the top of the steps, blowing the signal for everyone to make their way into the school, one class at a time. As Class 5A was filing up the steps, Mrs Froom said: 'Stop!' Everyone halted.

Mrs Froom beckoned with her finger and said: 'Miss Lacey!' Fenella went over to her. Mrs Froom said: 'I noticed that garment you are wearing when I spoke to you in the playground just now. It is not suitable as school uniform.'

'But, Mrs Froom—' said Fen.

'I've had enough answering back from you for one day!' snarled the deputy head. 'You will write out one hundred times, I MUST BE PROUD OF MY UNIFORM, and bring the lines to me first thing tomorrow morning. Meanwhile, you must remove that garment.'

'Here, Mrs Froom?'

'No, of course not! Go to the changing room and put on your gym T-shirt. And hurry!'

The rest of the class went on through the doors

and into the large tiled hallway, towards the door that led to the assembly hall.

Mrs Froom snapped: 'Get a move on, there! And no talking! Remember, this is a silent area.'

The main hallway of the school was one of several places which the head labelled silent areas. No talking was allowed, except during lunch break. Even discussing the latest announcements or regulations on the big notice board in the hallway was not permitted. Since the staff room led off the hallway, to the right of the main doors, there were always teachers coming and going, ready to tick you off and give you some sort of punishment if they caught you even whispering.

Fen got back into the assembly hall after changing, as Mr Maddox was finishing his list of announcements. He stopped in mid-sentence and looked down the hall at Fen.

'Miss Lacey!' he said sharply. Fen stopped. The head went on with heavy sarcasm: 'How good of you to favour us by joining our gathering today. But you are five minutes LATE!' He barked out the last word loudly. Fen was about to speak, when she saw Mrs Froom stand up and say something to the head. He nodded, and then frowned towards Fen, saying: 'Get into your place at once!'

Fen made her way into the row where Edward and Stass were sitting. 'You haven't missed anything,' whispered Stass. 'Just more announcements about drilling practice.'

Spencer's School was known for its emphasis on disciplined activities, particularly marching drills. Every class had to do them regularly, and each term there was a big display for the parents. This featured a top squad which did special drilling

8

movements. Kenneth and his friends were all in the squad, and scoffed at anybody who wasn't good enough to get into it.

Up on the platform, the teachers stood up. They were all wearing black gowns, and looked like some kind of funeral party. Mr Maddox was taller than all the rest of them, and he dominated the platform, standing at his lectern and gazing watchfully around the hall. He was tall and thin, with a white face and a small black moustache which he would sometimes finger proudly. His eyebrows were black too, and bushy, above the narrow, beady eyes that always seemed to be searching for something to find fault with.

When the teachers stood, everyone in the hall got to their feet. It was the signal for the singing of the school song, which was sung every morning at assembly.

The music teacher, Miss Jellinek, tall and wispy-haired, and wearing a faded flower-patterned dress under her gown, went across and sat down at a piano at the side of the stage. She played the opening chords, and the familiar chorus sounded:

'Hail, glorious Spencer's, our school of renown,
The pride of our nation, the jewel in its crown.
O Spencer's, you gave us our happiest days,
So let us rejoice now and sing in thy praise . . . '

When the song was over, Mr Maddox held up his hand and said: 'Before you go, I wish to tell the school that I shall be making a number of surprise visits to classrooms this week. I have noticed that pupils are becoming decidedly slack about tidiness. I want this to stop, at once. Do not discard wrapping paper on the floor, do not leave desks and chairs all higgledy-piggledy, but straighten them in regular rows. Make sure all blackboards are cleaned before you leave the classroom after each lesson, and put away all books and other equipment you have been using. I happened to go into the history room after school yesterday, and it was nothing short of disgraceful. I checked the timetable and saw that Class 4B had been the last occupants. They will all stay after school today and do litter duty in the playground for one hour. Very well – dismiss!'

'Again!' rapped Mr Farmer, the geography teacher.

Once more the class chanted together: 'Derwent, Swale, Ure, Nidd, Wharfe, Aire, Calder, Don.'

'Good,' said Mr Farmer. 'Now when it comes to exams, no one will be able to fault you on the order of the eastern rivers of England, in Yorkshire. And just so you will make sure to remember them, I want you each to write them down.'

'As if I hadn't got enough writing to do, with all those lines tonight,' said Fen to Stass.

'What was that, Fenella?' asked Mr Farmer sharply.

'Nothing, sir.' Mr Farmer frowned. He had dark wavy hair and a jutting chin, and thought himself very handsome. Behind his back, people called him Farmer the Smarmer. Like the rest of the teaching staff at Spencer's, he believed that the only way to learn was to recite things over and over again. It didn't mean you actually understood anything, but at least you could trot out the answers to exam questions.

At the end of the lesson, Mr Farmer said: 'Now,

remember what the headmaster said about leaving the room tidy. Straighten those desks! Tidy those books! Clean that board! Let's have a little school spirit, shall we? I gather we have a new pupil joining your class tomorrow, and we want to set him a good example, don't we?' He paused, then said again: 'Don't we?'

The class chorused: 'Yes, Mr Farmer.'

As people began tidying up, there was a buzz of chatter about the new pupil. Who was he? Why was he suddenly joining the class in the middle of term?

'Silence!' said Mr Farmer. 'That will do – you may take them away to their next unfortunate teacher, Kenneth.'

'Thank you, sir. Class, dismiss!' As they began to file out, Kenneth stayed behind to ask Mr Farmer about the new arrival.

'Expelled?!' Caroline's eyes were wide, as they stood in a huddle at the edge of the main steps during the morning break.

'That's what Mr Farmer told me,' said Kenneth.

'What for?' Simon asked.

'For being a troublemaker. That's what Mr Farmer said.'

'He'd better not try making trouble here,' said Simon. 'The Mad Ox will soon clobber him if he does.'

'Yes, Mr Maddox will certainly know how to deal with him.' Kenneth didn't use the headmaster's nickname. He believed in being respectful to the teachers – you never knew when they might be within earshot. His attitude seemed to pay off, and he was often held up as an example to the other pupils. He was well aware that it had a lot to do with his father's financial help to the school.

But Kenneth's high standing with the teachers didn't impress Fen, who came up to join in the conversation.

'Who will the Mad Ox know how to deal with, Kenny?' she asked.

Kenneth looked at her disdainfully. 'The new boy who's starting tomorrow. His name's Redman.'

'He was expelled from his last school,' said Caroline. 'For troublemaking.'

'Sounds interesting,' said Fen.

'Well, personally, I think we can do without that sort of person at Spencer's,' said Kenneth.

'So do I,' Caroline echoed. 'And anyway, you made a lot of trouble yourself, with that shirt you were wearing.'

'The rules only say *blue*, they don't say what kind of blue,' said Fen. She still resented having to remove the turquoise-blue satin shirt, which her mother had bought on one of her frequent shopping sprees to the classy London stores.

'Personally, I think the whole idea of uniforms is that people should look the same, not different,' Kenneth said.

'OK, Kenny, I'll make you a shirt like mine, if you want, then you'll look like me!'

There was a chuckle from Edward, who had come up to them and was standing between Fen and Kenneth. Kenneth stuck out his elbow and turned suddenly towards Edward, jabbing him in the chest. Edward gave a cry of pain.

'Oh, sorry,' said Kenneth with a sneering smile. 'I didn't see you there, Edward. You're so small.'

Simon and Caroline laughed.

'You'll have to watch out, or someone will tread on you,' said Kenneth, and he turned away and walked off, followed by his cronies.

Edward rubbed his sore chest. He and Fen both realized there was no point in starting another fight with Kenneth and the rest of them. They were in enough trouble after the last one.

After school, they went to collect some cleaning materials from Mr Grimley in the caretaker's room, which was just beside the staff room, off the main hallway.

'In trouble again, are you?' said Mr Grimley sympathetically. 'Come in, I'll find you something.'

They always liked going into Mr Grimley's room. It was like a combination of an Aladdin's cave and a jumble sale. There were shelves of paint tins, and brushes in jars, and racks of carpentry tools, and a workbench with a vice on it, and boxes of light bulbs, and saws and garden rakes and brooms.

But best of all, behind a curtain on a special shelf behind the door, were several bottles on horizontal stands. Each of them had a tiny ship inside, mainly galleons with full billowing sails, on a painted blue sea. Making these was Mr Grimley's hobby – but he liked to keep it a secret from the teachers. Sometimes, if you knocked at his door, he would say: 'Wait!' and then when he said: 'All right, come in,' you would see a green cloth covering something on his workbench, and some tools and glue and a paintbox beside it.

Once, Fen had gone straight in after knocking and seen the ship Mr Grimley was making. He was annoyed at her, until he saw her expression of amazed delight. Then quite shyly he showed her the ship, and the others behind the curtain. But he made her promise not to tell any of the staff.

Mr Grimley almost trembled at the mention of the name of Mr Maddox or Mrs Froom. He seemed to be afraid they would fire him if they got the chance, because they were often heard telling him off or shouting at him to hurry.

He gave Fen a mop, and handed a bucket to Stass, and a few cloths and some cleaning fluid to Edward. Then he got out two black rubbish bags and handed them over too.

'Put them round the back in the rubbish yard, and tie them up tightly. The head is always on at me about how untidy that yard gets. I'm sure some of the kids come and mess it about on purpose.'

'Thanks, Mr Grimley,' said Fen. 'We'll bring back the mop and stuff.'

Cleaning the locker room was a mucky job. It smelt of dirty socks, and the floor was streaked with dried mud.

'I'd like to get a hose and spray this whole place with a jet of sludge, flood it out, and then push off for ever,' said Stass.

'You'd certainly have to push off for ever pretty quick,' Fen laughed. 'The Mad Ox would murder you.'

'And expel you as well,' said Edward.

'Like that boy who got expelled from his last school,' said Stass. 'He must have done something dreadful.'

'Perhaps he'll do the same thing here,' said Fen. 'It would certainly liven the place up a bit, whatever it was.'

2

Ricky Redman took two oranges from his duffel bag and slung the bag on his shoulder. He started to juggle the oranges in front of him as he began to walk to his new school. He would have cycled there, but his bike had got a bit bent when he tried to do the Wall of Death ride on the wall at the back of the supermarket car park.

He juggled happily all along his own road, but as he turned the corner into Harcourt Street he nearly collided with Mr McArdle, who was out with his dog, Sandy. Mr McArdle was standing gazing around him, as though quite unaware of what Sandy was doing squatting at the edge of the pavement. As Ricky stepped quickly aside, one of the oranges fell on to Sandy's head. The dog gave a startled yelp.

Mr McArdle, in a voice as startled as his dog's, cried: 'Watch where you're going, laddie!'

'Sorry!' said Ricky, picking up the orange and walking quickly on his way. He carried on juggling till he came to the top of the road that led to Spencer's School. At the far end of the road he could see the school's large ornamental iron gates standing open between big brick pillars.

Inside the gates, in the middle of the asphalt playground, stood a statue on a square stone plinth. Beyond the statue, Ricky could see the wide steps that led up to the arched entrance of the big brick building. As he looked at the groups of boys and

15

girls in blue uniforms gathered in the playground, he wondered if he would find this place as boring as he had found his last school – the one which he had been asked to leave.

As he approached, he could see a tall boy with smoothed-down blond hair, standing with his arm leaning on the plinth of the statue, talking earnestly to a girl with black curly hair who was gazing up at him. Ricky wondered what they were saying. In fact, they were talking about *him* . . .

'I can't think why they allowed him to come here,' said Caroline.

'I expect they thought the discipline would do him good,' said Kenneth. 'He won't get far with any rebellious tactics here at Spencer's.'

Caroline touched his arm and said: 'Hey! Do you think that's him there?'

She pointed towards the gate, at the boy with spiky red hair, wearing glasses, who was standing gazing around the playground.

'Could be,' said Kenneth. 'Let's go over.'

As they went towards him, they saw the new boy starting to talk to Stass. Stass saw them approaching and whispered something to Ricky, who nodded and smiled.

'Hello, Kenny,' said Stass.

'Hello, Kebab-Face,' said Kenneth. The two glared at each other.

'What's *your* name?' asked Caroline.

'Ricky. Ricky Redman.'

Kenneth gave a wink and nod to Caroline.

'What's up?' Ricky asked.

'Oh . . . nothing, really,' said Kenneth. 'It's just

that we heard you left your last school . . . involuntarily.'

'I was expelled, if that's what you mean.'

'Tough luck,' said Fen.

'Not really.' Ricky smiled. 'I didn't like the place.'

'I doubt if you'll find Spencer's much of an improvement,' said Fen with a laugh.

'It all depends whether he wants to fit in or not,' said Kenneth, 'and I certainly don't think those clothes fit in with Spencer's standards!'

Ricky said nothing. He simply looked from one to the other of them, as if sizing them up. He seemed perfectly relaxed. His father had told him the school rules said blue uniform, so he had worn a blue T-shirt, jeans and his denim anorak. That was uniform enough, he thought.

Kenneth didn't know quite how to react to Ricky's silence. He decided to show off. 'I'm a school prefect, you know,' he said, '*and* the captain of the school cricket team. Do you like cricket?'

'Not much,' said Ricky.

'What's your best game, then?'

'I play a bit of pool.'

Fen chuckled, but Kenneth wasn't amused. 'Not quite what I had in mind, actually,' he said. 'But I suppose it's not easy for you, with the eyesight problem.'

'Eyesight problem?' Ricky looked puzzled.

'The glasses,' said Kenneth.

'Oh, those,' said Ricky. 'They're spectacles, not glasses.'

'Same thing.'

'Not exactly. I need them for my eyes all right, but they're not like ordinary glasses. These spectacles let me see backwards as well as forwards, without turning my head.'

'I don't believe you.'

'Right, I'll turn away and look out through the gate, like this.'

Ricky realized that they were all facing away from the school, so they had not seen the figure of Mrs Froom come out through the main doors and stand looking out at the playground from the top of the steps. He had glimpsed her there before he turned away.

'Well, what do you see?' asked Stass eagerly.

'I see a tall woman with grey hair, standing on the top of the steps.'

The others turned towards the school. Sure enough, there on the steps stood the deputy head.

The group all turned back to look at Ricky. He was still standing gazing unconcernedly out of the gate.

'Say, those must be quite some glasses!' said Stass.

'It's a trick,' grunted Kenneth.

'A trick,' agreed Caroline, nodding vigorously.

Ricky shrugged. 'It works,' he said.

'All right, let me try them on.' Kenneth reached out his hand.

Ricky waved him away. 'They only work for *me*.' He saw Stass looking at him open-mouthed. Ricky winked, and Stass grinned back at him, realizing how Ricky had fooled them.

The alarm bell sounded.

'A fire!' said Ricky. 'Well, that will keep us out of school for a bit.'

'That is the school bell,' said Kenneth scornfully. 'Come on, 5A, line up. Hurry!'

As they formed into lines, Ricky asked: 'Who is that dragon at the top of the steps?'

'Mrs Froom, the deputy head,' said Stass. 'And dragon is the right word for her.'

'Who's that chattering?' snapped Mrs Froom, stamping down the steps and coming across to 5A's group. She stood with her hands on her hips, glaring down at them.

'You're the new boy, are you?' she said to Ricky.

'Yes, miss.'

'Not "Yes, miss"! You say "Yes, Mrs Froom". Is that clear?'

'Yes, Mrs Froom.'

'The headmaster would like a word with you, immediately after assembly. And I want no more chattering from this class, or you'll suffer for it!' She marched away up to the top of the steps, where she turned and produced a referee's whistle. She blew a shrill blast on it, and the lines began to move inside.

As Mr Maddox gave out his usual list of announcements, complaints, threats and punishments, Ricky looked around the hall. On shelves along one wall there were rows of gleaming cups and shields – sporting trophies for matches within the school and victories against other schools.

On the wall at the back of the stage was a painting of a stern-looking, whiskered man with an old-fashioned style of coat and collar and tie. It was the same man as the one whose statue stood in the centre of the playground: Sir Rumbelow Spencer, a local factory owner who had founded the school many years ago. Then it had been a private preparatory school, but now it was maintained by government grant.

It was officially run by a board of governors, but in fact they all did what Mr Maddox told them. They were people who liked his ideas of rigid discipline, and his attempts to model the school on the old public schools.

Mr Maddox would like to have been head of one of those, but in the ten years since he left the army and went into teaching, he had only succeeded in becoming headmaster of Spencer's. So he tried to make that into his idea of a traditional school, ruled by a system of harsh routines and punishments.

Ricky was aware of some heads in the rows in front turning towards him, and turning back to whisper to companions. The story of The New Boy Who Had Been Expelled had obviously got around. When Ricky caught the eye of anyone who turned to stare at him, he stared back and waggled his ears up and down, which made his spectacles jiggle on his nose.

He looked at the stage. Wouldn't it be a great idea to take the oranges out of his duffel bag and go up there and show them his juggling act? He had to admit to himself that it wouldn't be such a good idea – certainly not on his first day.

He noticed a large shield below the portrait of Sir Rumbelow, with a picture of a sailing ship on it. He turned to Stass beside him and asked: 'What does that ship mean, on the shield?'

'It doesn't mean anything – it's just the school badge.'

But Edward, beside Stass, leaned forward and whispered: 'Actually, Spencer can mean a kind of mast on a ship, so the Mad Ox chose a ship for the school's coat of arms.'

Stass told Ricky: 'This is Edward. He's a know-all.'

'No, I'm not,' said Edward. 'I just like facts. When I've got enough facts, I'm going to put them all in a book.'

'What will it be called?'

'*A Dictionary of the Entire Planet*, in fifteen volumes.'

'You'd better start soon,' said Ricky, 'or you'll never get it finished.'

'Oh, I *have* started,' said Edward. 'I've got as far as A for Acid Rain.'

'Be quiet there!' hissed Kenneth loudly, turning round from the row in front.

'I'd say A stands for Ass, in his case,' Ricky whispered to Stass.

Kenneth frowned. 'What was that you said?'

But just then there was a scraping of chairs, and everyone stood up. The opening chords of the school song came from Miss Jellinek's piano, and Ricky listened in some surprise as the whole hall re-sounded with singing:

'Hail glorious Spencer's, our school of renown,
The pride of our nation, the jewel in its
    crown . . . '

In the wood-panelled headmaster's study, with annual school photographs in frames round the walls, Mr Maddox sat at a huge leather-topped desk, his hands clasped in front of him. From under his bushy eyebrows, he frowned at Ricky, who was standing just in front of the desk.

21

'As it is your first day here, Redman, I will over-look the scruffy clothes.'

Mr Maddox went on to tell him to make sure that he got a proper jacket, and wore grey flannel trousers, and a shirt, and a school tie. Then the headmaster asked sarcastically: 'And do you call those things on your feet shoes?'

Ricky looked down at his well-worn trainers. 'Well, that's what they are, sir.'

'They are not what we call shoes at Spencer's, boy!' barked the head. 'Here you will wear proper black shoes. Is that clear?'

'Yes, sir.'

Mr Maddox went on to say that a uniform should be worn with pride, and a Spencer's boy or girl should stand out from the common herd. People knew that here was someone who was clean, tidy and well-mannered, with respect for adults, and no wild ways. That was what the tradition of Spencer's meant, and why the school spirit was what they tried to foster.

The headmaster paused, gazing at Ricky. Then he said: 'Redman – I regard you as a challenge. That's why I said we would take you in here at Spencer's. When we have gone to work on you, you'll fit in like all the rest – a Spencer's pupil, with all that means. Right – dismiss!'

Ricky picked up his duffel bag from the floor beside him, and turned and went to the door. As he opened it, he heard the head's voice bark:

'Stand up straight, Redman! Shoulders back! Don't shamble! You'll never be in the marching squad with a walk like that!'

Ricky thought he'd rather run the marathon backwards in clogs through a field of cowpats than join the marching squad; but he thought it wiser just to say 'Yes, sir,' and leave the room.

The room beside the headmaster's was Mrs Froom's. The door was open, and when she saw Ricky come out of the head's study, she got up from her desk and stepped briskly towards him. She looked at a clipboard she was holding, and said:

'You are in Class 5A, Redman. They are at present in the Columbus Room, for Mr Farmer's geography class. Along the corridor, third door on the right.'

'Thank you, miss,' said Ricky – then, seeing her laser eyes glare at him, he said: 'I mean . . . thank you, Mrs Froom.'

'That's better,' said the deputy head. 'Off you go!'

Ricky moved off down the corridor, past the pictures of school teams and marching squads that lined the walls. At the third door on the right he stopped. The word COLUMBUS was painted in firm black lettering on the green door. Ricky peered through the panes of glass in the top half of the door.

He saw Mr Farmer on the platform, conducting what seemed to be a sort of question-and-answer chant. Ricky could hear it easily through the door: as well as believing that things could only be learned by reciting lists, Mr Farmer also thought the recitation had to be as loud as possible.

'The capital of France is . . .' boomed Mr Farmer, waving his arms.

The class all shouted: 'PARIS.'

'The capital of Spain is . . .'

'MADRID.'

'The capital of. . . .' Mr Farmer stopped as Ricky

opened the door and came into the room. 'Yes?' said the teacher sharply.

'The head told me to come here,' said Ricky.

'Oh, you're the new boy, are you?'

'That's right,' said Ricky.

'That's right, *sir*,' said Mr Farmer.

'Sir,' said Ricky.

'And your name is . . . ?'

'Ricky Redman.'

'Sir!' snapped the teacher.

'But I'm not,' said Ricky.

'Not what?'

'Not Sir Ricky Redman . . . sir.'

Ricky heard a stifled laugh. It came from Stass, who was sitting nearby. There were some murmurs from the rest of the class, but they soon stopped as Mr Farmer shouted: 'Silence!'

'The first thing you must learn, Redman,' said Mr Farmer icily, 'is that if there are any jokes to be made in this classroom, *I* make them. Is that clear?'

'Yes, sir.'

'Very well. Now sit down and pay attention.'

Ricky looked around, and saw Stass pointing to a spare place next to him. He sat down at the desk, and whispered: 'Thanks.' Stass grinned a welcome.

The chanting of the capitals of Europe went on. Ricky joined in with the ones he knew. For the others, he just opened his mouth silently. Meanwhile, he looked around the room.

The walls had orangy-brown tiles from the floor up to the window ledges, and above that they were painted a dusty cream colour. There were maps and charts pinned to the walls, and in one corner on a table stood a large globe of the world.

Ricky thought of all the capitals they were chanting, and felt sure that one day he would visit them
all. If he got really good at his juggling, maybe he
could join a circus, or go on tour as part of a cabaret
act.

His father wouldn't mind. He let Ricky do more
or less what he liked, especially after Ricky's mother
had left home a year ago with that computer salesman. Now Ricky and his father had got used to a
pleasant, relaxed home life. They both met for the
simple meals they made together, but otherwise
went their own ways.

Ricky's father worked in the packing department
of a local department store, but spent all his spare
time with his pigeons in the loft he had built in the
back yard. Ricky was always either practising his
juggling, or riding his bike around the town and
out into the countryside, where it was easier to
practise his cycling tricks.

It had been rash, he realized now, to build a
bonfire at the back of the school bike sheds to show
off his trick of riding up a ramp and over the flames.
How was he to know the wind would suddenly get
gusty and strong, and blow the fire towards the
sheds?

There wasn't much left of the bike sheds by the
time the fire brigade had put out the flames, but
Ricky thought there had been too much fuss about
the whole business. After all, the bicycles had
mostly been OK, even if they were drenched.

Ricky's father had done his best to defend him,
but Mrs Deakin, the head teacher, said Ricky had
been mixed up in too many escapades, and this was
really the last straw. She herself had suggested that
Spencer's might be the best place for Ricky.

The schools were known to be bitter rivals – at least, their head teachers were. Mrs Deakin thought Mr Maddox's methods harsh and old-fashioned, while he regarded her school as having a wishy-washy, sloppy attitude to discipline.

Mr Maddox was only too glad to take Ricky, in spite of the fire episode. He was pleased to know that Mrs Deakin had to admit failure with a pupil. Mrs Deakin, on the other hand, felt that Ricky might be a lot more than Spencer's could handle.

'I didn't hear you, Redman.' Mr Farmer's voice broke into Ricky's daydreaming about new bike tricks and juggling acts.

He realized the chanting had stopped and Mr Farmer was staring at him. He gazed back at the teacher without speaking.

'I said, I didn't hear you,' Mr Farmer repeated. 'Now, all on your own this time: the capital of Finland is . . . '

'Helsinki,' said Ricky.

'Helsinki, *sir*!'

'Helsinkissa,' said Ricky, in one long word. Beside him, Stass chuckled. Mr Farmer frowned.

'If you are to be a pupil here at Spencer's,' he said, 'you should understand that the first thing we all have to learn in this world is respect for our elders and betters. Respect. What must we learn?'

The class, led by Kenneth, replied: 'Respect, sir!'

'And respect,' Mr Farmer went on, 'means not only respect for those who lead and guide you in the present, but for the illustrious people who have established the great tradition which has made Spencer's School the noble example it is today. People like our founder, the great merchant and

26

philanthropist Sir Rumbelow Spencer. Does everyone know what a philanthropist is?'

'A stamp collector, sir?' asked Ricky innocently.

'Wrong!' snapped Mr Farmer. 'That's a philatelist. A philanthropist is someone who does good works for the benefit of the community. Redman – did you notice the statue as you came in at the gates of the school?'

'Statue, sir?'

'Yes, statue, boy! You could hardly miss it. It's up on a stone plinth, right in front of you.'

'Oh, yes, sir. I thought it was just one of the teachers standing up to have a look around.'

The members of the class glanced at one another. No one had dared to talk to Mr Farmer like that before. Or to any other teacher, for that matter. They waited in breathless silence to hear how he would react.

Mr Farmer chose to be sarcastic. 'You thought it was a teacher, did you? Then perhaps, Redman, you ought to get your glasses changed.'

There was a pause, then Ricky said seriously: 'I don't think you should make fun of a person's disability, sir.'

Mr Farmer gazed at Ricky, uncertain what to say. Ricky gazed back. The rest of the class stared in frozen silence, as though fixed by some sudden magic spell.

Mr Farmer decided to back away from an argument which could seem to put him in the wrong. He said sharply: 'It was your attitude I was criticizing, Redman. I had certainly no intention of commenting on your disability, or your glasses.'

'Spectacles, sir,' said Ricky.

'Very well then, spectacles!' said Mr Farmer.

'Now, I think it's time we went on with our geography lesson. The capital of Sweden is . . . '

'STOCKHOLM!' the class roared, with Ricky this time shouting as loudly as the rest.

3

During the lunch break, Stass and Edward had been told by the head to sweep the hallway, after he had caught them running in the corridor. Fen was having the school lunch.

So Ricky went out into the playground on his own to eat the sandwiches he had made for himself. He sat down on a low wall in the corner of the playground and opened up the plastic bag. The sandwiches had got a bit lopsided being carried about, but Ricky thought they looked very tasty all the same.

The slices of thick brown curranty buttered bread had wedged between them a layer of peanut butter, a layer of strawberry jam, some slices of cold sausage and a dollop of cottage cheese. Ricky had to open his mouth as wide as he could in order to get a proper bite at it all.

He had finished one sandwich, and was just washing it down with a can of fizzy lemon before starting on the next, when he saw people starting to come out of the school entrance after their meal. Among them were Kenneth and Caroline and Simon. Seeing him sitting on the wall, they came across the playground towards him.

'What's that, a home-made Whopper?' said Caroline, pointing at the sandwich.

'Looks more like a squashed hamster,' said Kenneth.

Ricky didn't say anything. It would have been

hard to speak anyway, since he'd just taken a huge bite of his second sandwich and was chewing happily.

'I'm going to give you a bit of advice, Redman,' said Kenneth. Ricky looked at him inquiringly and went on chewing.

'Remember what Mr Farmer said about respect,' Kenneth continued. 'He didn't mean just the teachers, you know. We've got prefects in this school, and I'm one of them. So just you watch it, new boy!'

Ricky returned Kenneth's glare without blinking. Then, without taking his eyes from Kenneth's, he put the sandwich to his mouth, took another big bite, and began chewing slowly and noisily.

'I said, watch it,' said Kenneth angrily. 'But if you're not careful, you won't be able to watch anything by the time we've finished with you.'

Suddenly he reached forward and snatched the spectacles from Ricky's face. Ricky made a grab for them, but Kenneth stepped back. Simon seized Ricky's arm and twisted it behind his back. Kenneth was holding up the spectacles.

Ricky jabbed his elbow into Simon's stomach, and Simon gasped and swore, but still held his arm.

'Don't try to mix it with *us*, new boy!' said Kenneth. He dropped the spectacles and then put his foot just above them on the ground, ready to stamp on them. Ricky stayed still. He needed the spectacles, and he knew Kenneth would smash them if he resisted.

'You think you're a smart little sod, don't you?' said Kenneth with a sneer. 'That trick you played, pretending you could see backwards – well, it didn't fool *me*. And I don't care for people who try to play tricks on me, see?'

'Go on, Kenneth, tread on the glasses!' said Caroline gleefully. 'He won't be able to see to play tricks then.'

'Yeah – tread on them!' said Simon.

'No, I'm going to let Speccy Four-Eyes off, just this once,' said Kenneth. 'We'll make him pick them up, instead.'

'Go on, kneel down!' said Simon, pushing Ricky to the ground. Ricky snatched the spectacles up and put them on. He started to stand up, but Simon pushed him down again.

'I didn't say get up!' he snapped.

'Hey, is this a fight?' said a tall, toothy girl, coming over to the group.

'Yes, and Kenneth won!' said Caroline smugly.

Kenneth smiled. 'Yes, I won. You can get up now, new boy.'

Ricky scrambled to his feet and dusted himself down.

'Yes, you won,' he said. 'But that was only the first round.' He stared hard at Kenneth.

The fair-haired prefect gave a sneering smile. 'Get lost, Four-Eyes!' he said, and turned and walked off, followed by Caroline, Simon and the toothy girl, who was chattering eagerly in admiration.

Ricky watched them go. He wasn't afraid of bullies like Kenneth – but he knew you couldn't get the better of them by brute force. Ricky preferred more subtle kinds of revenge – and he was sure he would find something for Kenneth and his cronies before long.

He turned his back on the playground and put

his duffel bag on the wall. He got the two oranges out, and began juggling.

'Hey, that's really good!' said Fen, coming over to him.

'I can nearly do it with three.'

'I saw you talking to Kenneth and his lot, just as I came out,' Fen said. 'What was he on about?'

'Just trying to show me who's boss around here. But don't worry, I can get back at *him*!'

'Well, count me in, if you want any help – he and that Simon are real thugs. The trouble is, Kenneth is a teacher's pet too. The teachers always take his side.'

'Then we'll have to get back at *them*, as well.'

'You certainly got the better of old Farmer the Smarmer, with all that stuff about disability. He was dead embarrassed.'

'People shouldn't sneer at spectacles.'

'No – they should be like a badge, so people would be proud to wear them. Hey, that's given me an idea!'

'What's that?'

'Wait and see – I'll show you tomorrow.'

'But darling, *why* do you want my old glasses? Your eyes are perfectly all right.' Fen's mother was painting her nails at her bedroom table.

'I'd just like to borrow them. One of the lenses is broken anyway, and you've got new ones now.'

'All right, I'll see if I can find them.'

'They're in the second drawer down, on the right. Under your stockings.'

'Really dear, you shouldn't rummage, it's not polite. Ah yes, you're right, there they are. I'd forgotten they were red. I must have got them to go

32

with that red outfit I wore at Mrs Thrimbleton-Thing's charity ball. How too too garish!'

'I'll take out the lenses and they'll look great on me.'

'Oh, the fashions of the young! Mind you, we had some fairly far-out styles in my day, too. I remember the dress they called the Sack . . . '

Fenella slipped out of the room before her mother could get launched on one of her rambling trips down Memory Lane.

His father wasn't around when Ricky got home. He had a look in the pigeon loft in the back yard, but he wasn't there. Perhaps he was out at the allotment. Ricky got a frozen pizza out and put it ready to go into the microwave.

He thought about the day at Spencer's. It seemed a bit of an oddball place, but no worse than the last school. At least he'd got through the first day without being thrown out!

He decided not to worry about it. One day at a time, that was the answer. Meanwhile, there were important things to do. Ricky took the two oranges from his bag, picked another one from the wooden fruit bowl on the kitchen table, and began to juggle.

The next morning at assembly, the school song was sung with the same roaring and tuneless vigour as usual. Ricky wondered if he'd be able to bear listening to that row every morning of the school term. Perhaps he could make up some new words to it and sing them himself. It would relieve the boredom, and no one would notice in the middle of all that noise.

After the singing, Mr Maddox made announcements about the school timetable, and told Class 3A that they would all have an hour's detention after school because a group of them had been seen 'larking about' at the bus stop, by Mrs Froom.

He also wanted volunteers for a project to clean the statue of Sir Rumbelow Spencer: names could be put on a list on the school notice board. Then he said:

'Finally, I'm sure you will all be pleased and honoured to know that we have been invited to make a series of school outings to the stately home of Lord and Lady Fuddlecombe. Your history teacher, Miss Grenfell, will be your guide, and I shall be able to tell you all in advance about what you will see, since of course I have been a frequent guest at Fuddlecombe Manor.'

'He went there twice with the choir to sing carols,' said Stass to Ricky.

'Hark the Herald Mad Ox sings!' said Ricky.

They both stifled a laugh, and saw Kenneth look along the row and glare at them.

In the morning break, Ricky went off to the corner of the playground where he had sat yesterday. He wanted to practise his juggling. Last night he had almost perfected the three-oranges routine. Even his father was impressed.

Fen came across to him. 'You've done it!' she said admiringly. 'Three oranges at once – that's great.'

'Thanks,' said Ricky.

'Now I've got something to show *you*.' She held up the red spectacles. 'Remember what I said: they should be like a badge.'

She put them on. The red glassless frames went

up into points at the side. They gave her an air of flashy confidence.

'Terrific!' said Ricky. 'You look like one of those television people.'

Fen was pleased. She said showily: 'Good evening! And my first guest tonight is Ricky Redman, the amazing orange-juggler. Take it away, Ricky!'

Just then Stass appeared. 'Fen, you've got glasses!'

'All the better to see you with, Stass.'

'They look good. Have your eyes gone off?'

'No, it's sort of a badge.'

'Like for a gang?'

'Yes.'

'I've got some dark glasses at home. Can I join?'

Fen looked at Ricky. 'Sure,' said Ricky. 'If you agree, Fen?'

'I agree.'

Edward came over.

Stass said: 'Ricky and Fen have just formed a gang, and when I bring my spectacles, I'll be in it too.'

Edward looked disappointed. Then his face brightened as he said: 'I've got some old spectacles of my grandmother's. She's just got some new ones. Can I join? I could write out the Dictionary of Rules!'

'You're in!' said Ricky, grinning. 'We need someone to keep the records, as well as do the rules.'

'Records of what?'

'Of all the gang's interests and activities. And enemies!' he added darkly.

'I could write them in code,' said Edward.

'Good thinking,' said Ricky. 'Now, we'll all meet here tomorrow, at the same time. With our spectacles. They're our badge of membership, as Fen says. Our special sign.'

'What's this little huddle all about?' Kenneth had come up to the group without their noticing him.

'Nothing,' said Stass.

Edward said: 'We were just talking about ... er ... about ...'

'Oranges!' said Fen, pointing at the three oranges which Ricky had put down on the wall beside him.

'Really?' said Kenneth. 'Well, it's nice of you to share them like this.'

He leaned forward, picked up one of the oranges, and began peeling it.

'Here!' said Fen, stepping towards Kenneth. Ricky put his hand on her arm.

'Hold it,' he said out of the corner of his mouth. 'This is a matter for the gang. We'll get our revenge.'

Kenneth looked surprised that they hadn't tried to stop him. He was obviously an even fiercer figure than he thought. He laughed, and swaggered off, biting into the orange as he went.

Ricky smiled, and began juggling the two remaining oranges.

That afternoon, Ricky had his first class with Miss Grenfell, the history teacher. Her room was called the King Charles Room, and had a big portrait above the blackboard, showing the King with his long black curly wig.

There were other pictures of kings and queens around the walls, for Miss Grenfell was an ardent fan of royal families, past and present, and had once met Princess Anne. The 'meeting' actually was only a case of Miss Grenfell handing the Princess a plate of biscuits in the tea tent at a country gymkhana, but the way Miss Grenfell told it, you would think they practically had a four-course meal together.

Miss Grenfell was tall and slim, and had a carefully shaped hair-do with flecks of blonde in its generally bronze colour. Today she wore a stylish suit of dark grey, which looked rather like a man's business suit – except for the lacy frills of the white blouse in front.

'Today,' Miss Grenfell told the class, 'we are going to talk about the history of Fuddlecombe Manor, the stately home which Lord and Lady Fuddlecombe have so graciously invited us to visit. We may even be privileged to meet His Lordship and Her Ladyship themselves, so we must learn how to conduct ourselves properly, mustn't we?'

Cynthia Grenfell had a gushing voice, and her laugh was a kind of in-and-out snorting, like the noise a restless horse makes. In fact, she actually rode horses, and kept one of her own in a riding stable just on the western edge of the town. There was much speculation about Miss Grenfell's romances – but little definite information. But this didn't prevent her from getting the nickname 'Grenthia Sinful'.

A snuffly child called Sharon sneezed loudly.

'Now there we are,' said Miss Grenfell. 'A perfect example of learning how to conduct ourselves in society – or rather, how not to. What should you do when you sneeze, Sharon?'

Sharon paused, puzzled – then said: 'Say "Bless you!" miss.'

'No, no, no, you silly girl – it's other people who say "Bless you". *You* should say: "I beg your pardon".'

Sharon said with a snuffle: 'Yes, miss' – then sneezed again.

Ricky called out in a loud voice: 'Bless you!'

Fen took up the cry: 'Bless you!' So did Stass, and then Edward.

Miss Grenfell snapped: 'Be quiet! That's enough blessings. I want to hear what Sharon has to say.'

'I beg your pardon, miss.'

'Good.'

'Does that apply to belching too, miss?' asked Ricky.

'Well, I suppose so – but I trust we would all be genteel enough not to belch at all, or at least to do so discreetly enough not to be heard.'

'What about other noises, miss?' asked Ricky. 'I mean, what about—'

'That will do!' Miss Grenfell cut in sharply. 'I appreciate your keenness to learn, er . . . Ricky, is it?'

'Yes, miss. Ricky Redman.'

'Good, well just listen for a little while, please, Ricky, and we'll get on with the lesson. You all heard Mr Maddox this morning. It is a great honour for us to go to such an ancient house, where they say that indeed King Charles himself once slept.'

Edward held his hand up.

'Yes?' said Miss Grenfell.

'What do we do if we see a ghost, miss?'

Ricky muttered: 'You tell him, "*I* can see through *you*!"'

'That will do!' said Miss Grenfell sharply. 'You will not be seeing any ghosts.'

'There's no such thing, is there, Miss Grenfell?' said Kenneth.

'Of course not,' said the teacher.

'I heard there was one in a school once,' said Stass.

'Nonsense!' said Miss Grenfell.

'Only fools and twits believe in ghosts,' said Kenneth.

Ricky, his hand over his mouth, began to make a low moaning sound, a kind of 'Ooooooh-aaaaaah' that rose and fell like a slow wave.

Beside him, Stass grinned, and said: 'Listen, miss! What was that noise?' Ricky stopped.

Miss Grenfell said: 'What noise? I heard nothing. Now, stop chattering . . . ' Just then, Ricky began to moan again.

'There it is again!' said Stass. The sound rose and fell.

'Yes, there it is!' snapped Miss Grenfell angrily. 'And I know who is making it!' She strode down the room to where Ricky and Stass were sitting. Her hand darted out and she took hold of Ricky's ear.

'Get up!' she said, pulling his ear. Ricky stood. The teacher let go of his ear and said; 'Now, go to the corner to the left of the blackboard, and stand there, facing the wall.'

Ricky left his desk and did as she said. Miss Grenfell strode back to the platform. 'Put your hands on your head,' she told Ricky. When he had done that, she said: 'Now you will stand like that for the rest of the lesson, and tomorrow you will come to me with a hundred lines written out: I MUST NOT MAKE SILLY NOISES IN CLASS. Is that clear?'

'Yes, Miss Grenfell,' said Ricky.

'Very well. Now, to return to our history. The

original Fuddlecombe Manor was built over seven hundred years ago . . . '

As Miss Grenfell talked about the history of the mansion and the ancestors of Lord Fuddlecombe, Edward began to daydream. Surely, in a place as old as that, he thought, there must have been *some* dramatic events: quarrels, feuds, even murders. And in such a history, there was almost always a ghost lurking about. He made up his mind to do some research of his own.

4

The next morning, at the break, Ricky, Fen, Stass and Edward all gathered at the corner of the playground for the showing of the spectacles. Ricky was already wearing his, and Fen was the first of the others to put hers on.

'Yes, they really look good,' said Ricky. 'Stass, how about yours?'

With a flourish, Stass took from his pocket a pair of sunglasses with red frames, and put them on.

'Stylish, eh?' he said proudly.

'Just what the well-dressed Mafia boss is wearing,' said Ricky. 'Yes, they're cool.'

'The glass gets darker and lighter according to the amount of sun,' said Stass. 'I borrowed them off my father. Well, sort of borrowed. He never uses them, so he won't even notice.'

'Now what about yours, Edward?' said Ricky.

Shyly, Edward took out of his pocket a pair of half-moon spectacles with a thin chain attached to them. He put the chain round his neck, and put the spectacles on.

'Dead right!' said Fen. 'Very scholastic.'

'Just what the trendy dictionary-writer is wearing,' said Ricky.

Edward grinned.

'I've just thought of something,' said Ricky. 'Fen's and Stass's spectacles both have red frames. Supposing we all had red frames? That would be a real special sign we were part of the gang.'

'I'm sure there's some red lacquer paint in the art room,' said Edward. 'We could borrow that, if Mrs Turner will let us.'

'Great,' said Ricky.

'Mrs Turner needn't even know,' said Fen. 'I can get it at the lunch break and return it later.'

'So, Edward, we'll paint spectacles at lunch time,' said Ricky. 'Then, we need to have a founding ceremony and swear everybody in. We can do that after school. OK?'

'Sure,' said Fen, and the others nodded.

'Where shall we go?' asked Edward.

'What about the old boiler house behind the school hall? Nobody goes in there.'

'Sounds good, Fen,' said Ricky. 'We could make it our headquarters. But could anyone see us going in and out?'

'The door is round in the yard where the rubbish bins are. Only the caretaker goes there, and the garbage collectors twice a week. It's very smelly.'

'All the better, it will keep the curious people away. What about the door, though? Is it locked up?'

'There's a padlock, and a bolt, I think,' said Stass. 'But the door is wooden, and probably rotting away. I'll take a look at it at lunch time, after we've painted the spectacles.'

The spectacle-painting was a bit more messy than they had expected. Fen extracted the small tin of lacquer from the art room when no one was there, together with a couple of brushes. They huddled in the corner of the playground and put the two pairs of spectacles on the wall. Fen said she'd paint

42

Ricky's spectacles, since his vision wasn't too sharp with them off.

But it wasn't easy to avoid getting splashes of paint on the lenses. There was a great deal of wiping with handkerchief tissues and shirtsleeves to get the lenses clean. Finally the job was done, and Ricky's red spectacles gleamed bright.

Ricky picked them up and put them on, then realized in panic that the paint was still tacky and wet.

'They're sticking to my nose and my ears!' he cried.

'Take them off carefully,' said Fen, reaching out and removing them gently.

'That was close,' said Ricky. 'They could have got stuck to my face for ever. What are you grinning at, Stass?'

'Nothing – it's just that there's a kind of red ring all around your eyes, like a racoon.'

'Give me a handkerchief.'

He snatched the handkerchief Edward was holding, and wiped his face with it. Unfortunately it was the handkerchief they had been using to dab the paint that had spilt on the lenses. Ricky ended up with his face more red-stained than before.

'How do I look now?' he asked. Silently, Fen handed him a small mirror.

'Wow!' said Ricky. 'It looks like war paint.'

'Maybe the whole gang should wear it,' said Stass. 'And we could have our own tribal war dance, too.' He began to do a few steps of the Greek dancing at which he was an expert.

'We can think about that later,' said Ricky. 'Right now, I must go and wash this paint off my face. See you later on.'

'I haven't painted my spectacles yet,' said Edward gloomily, as he watched Ricky go.

'Well,' said Stass quickly, 'I must go and check out that lock on the boiler house door. See you!' He walked smartly away, across the playground.

'Come on, Edward, I'll give you a hand,' said Fen. 'You hold them, and I'll paint.'

By the time they had finished, there was as much paint on Edward's fingers as on the spectacles.

'See!' said Fen. 'You can hold them by the chain till they dry.'

But Edward was staring at his fingers in alarm.

'I look as if I've got painted fingernails,' he moaned.

'Don't worry, they'll just think you're one of the girls!' Fen laughed.

Edward grunted, and moved off to wash, holding out the newly red spectacles dangling on their chain.

After school, Ricky saw Kenneth writing on a notice on the board.

'Putting your name down for the statue-cleaning?' said Kenneth. '*We* are.' He gestured to Caroline and Simon and two or three other cronies standing nearby.

'Maybe,' said Ricky.

'It might show a bit of the school spirit you don't seem to have demonstrated much so far,' Kenneth sneered. 'But judging by the state of your face in the playground at lunch time, I'd say it was you who needs cleaning, not the statue.'

The others laughed.

Ricky smiled pleasantly and said: 'I'm sure you'll make a wonderful job of cleaning up Sir Rumble-

Tum.' He had made up his mind that somehow he would see that the statue-cleaning by Kenneth's group didn't go quite according to plan.

The boiler house was a big square brick building attached to the back of the school, in a yard surrounded by a high brick wall. There were some battered-looking metal dustbins, and great piles of bulging black rubbish bags heaped up against the wall. Other bags were strewn around the yard, with gashes in their sides, and cans and paper and bones and cabbage stalks and other garbage scattered on the ground.

Mr Grimley the caretaker had asked the headmaster if they could get sturdy metal containers, or at least some more dustbins, but Mr Maddox didn't believe in spending money on things that didn't show. He liked boasting and showing off the school to parents and governors, and he certainly didn't see himself taking them on a tour of the garbage yard.

Mr Grimley did his best to tie up the black bags and stack them neatly, but he was always finding them strewn about and torn and spilling on the ground. He suspected some of the pupils might be doing it, or maybe a down-and-out scavenging for food.

What worried him most was that Mr Maddox had taken to looking in on the yard and then giving Mr Grimley a fierce telling-off. Last time, he had been really threatening.

'That yard's a disgrace!' he barked. 'I'm warning you, Grimley, if I see the yard in that disgusting state again, I'm going to have to get rid of you. It's just not good enough. The job is getting too much for you, at your age.'

Mr Grimley knew the headmaster wanted to get rid of him, and the state of the garbage could be the ideal excuse. Short of patrolling the yard day and night, he couldn't see how he could stop it being messed around.

He had once told Fen he was afraid he wouldn't last there much longer because of the headmaster's hostility. The school was his life, and he couldn't imagine carrying on if he was sacked.

'We won't let him sack you, Mr Grimley,' Fen said. 'We'll support you.' But she very much feared there was little they could really do.

Fen was thinking about Mr Grimley as she picked her way through the scattered rubbish, across the yard to the boiler house. If the head found out they were using it, he could have an extra reason for firing Mr Grimley. They would just have to make sure that no one knew their secret meeting place.

Stass was already there, leaning against the wall of the boiler house and looking as if he owned it. Edward soon arrived, and then Ricky. He told them about Kenneth and the list of volunteers for the statue-cleaning.

'I've got an idea how we can make Kenneth's cleaning team look a right bunch of idiots,' said Ricky.

'Great!' said Fen. 'Tell us.'

'I'll tell you tomorrow,' said Ricky. 'I've got to do a bit of experimenting at home first, to see if my plan will work. Can we get into the boiler house, Stass?'

Stass stepped forward like a showman. 'For my first trick, ladies and gentlemen, I would like to show you my magic lock-opening act. As you can see, the padlock on this door is locked and the bolt is secure, so the door cannot be opened.'

'We'll have to find somewhere else then,' said Edward glumly.

'Not at all!' cried Stass. 'You will note that the wood around this metal bolt is flaking, so that if I stick this penknife between the metal and the wood, and give it a twist – hey presto!'

The metal came away from the wood, so that the whole bolt mechanism and the padlock were now fixed only to the door, and not to the doorpost.

'Now with one deft pull at the door,' said Stass, 'it's open sesame!' He pulled the door and it came open with a creak.

The others applauded.

'Nice work, Stass,' said Ricky.

'And the neat thing is,' Stass said, 'when we leave, we can put the screws back loosely in the holes, and it will look as if it's all bolted up again.'

'Perfect,' said Ricky. 'It will be our secret head-quarters. In we go!'

Inside, the boiler house was a wide, square room with grubby brick walls; it was quite high and had a dusty skylight in the roof. There was a large tank in the middle of one wall, with a network of pipes leading from it and running along the other walls and into the main building.

There was an empty bunker in one corner, with some scraps of coal on its floor. The place had been disused for some years, since the school got oil-fired heating. It was clearly a handy place to dump odds and ends, for there were a couple of ramshackle desks and some old chairs against one of the walls.

There were two wooden crates as well, and a

pile of empty cardboard boxes. An old telephone directory was on the floor too: Ricky noticed that the edges seemed to have been chewed up. Perhaps mice were the only inhabitants of the place – until now, with the arrival of the Red Spectacles Gang.

The four of them stood in the middle of the room, gazing around them. This dim and dusty place was the ideal hide-out.

'Now for the founding ceremony,' said Ricky. 'Let's all gather round and sit in a circle.'

They each dragged a chair or a crate to the centre of the room, so that they formed a circle. They all sat down except Edward, who gave his chair a quick dusting with his handkerchief. Then he sat.

There was a sharp cracking sound as one of the chair's legs broke in two, and the chair collapsed, letting Edward down with a bump on the floor.

'We won't count that as part of the ceremony,' said Ricky, grinning.

Stass helped Edward up, and Fen pulled a crate across for him to sit on. This time he didn't worry about dusting it.

'Well, who's going to start?' said Stass.

'You should, Ricky,' Fen said. 'You were the first one with the specs.' Stass and Edward agreed.

'OK,' said Ricky. He stood up, and held his right hand high in the air.

'Be it known to all and sundry,' he said in a booming voice, 'that we four are gathered here today to announce and swear our undying loyalty forever to that wonderful outfit, THE RED SPEC-TACLES GANG!'

'Hooray!' shouted Stass.

'Olé, olé, olé!' cried Fen.

'So let us all stand and clasp hands high.' They

48

stood and put their right hands up to form a four-sided arch. 'Now all together,' said Ricky. 'One, two, three, who are we?'

He paused, and they all shouted together: 'THE RED SPECTACLES GANG!'

They let their hands drop, laughing excitedly.

'We need a chant, like a team,' said Stass eagerly.

'Well, I was thinking about that,' said Ricky. He got a crumpled piece of paper out of his pocket and said: 'How about this?

'Stamp your feet, nod your head –
Spectacles on, and we all see red!'

'That's great!' said Stass.

'The idea is, we do the actions at the same time,' said Ricky.

'Let's try it,' said Fen.

'Right – we start with our spectacles off.' They all took off their spectacles. 'Now – one, two, three – go!'

They all chanted together:

'Stamp your feet, nod your head –
Spectacles on, and we all see red!'

'And again,' said Ricky.

They called out the chant once more, then began repeating it again and again, moving around in a circle as if they were doing some ritual dance. The pace got quicker and quicker. Finally Stass tried to include a tricky dance-step in his foot-stamping, tripped over himself and collapsed on to a crate.

They all stopped, happy and out of breath.

'I was wondering,' said Edward, 'do we wear our spectacles all the time now?'

'I don't think so,' said Ricky. 'Well, I have to wear mine to see properly, so nobody will think that's odd. But I think the rest of you should only put them on as a secret sign, when we're operating as a gang on some assignment, and when we're holding meetings, of course.'

'Pity,' said Fen, 'I rather fancy myself in these.'

'You'll get plenty of chances to wear them, when the gang really gets going,' said Ricky.

'I tell you what we need as well as a chant,' said Stass. 'A mascot. Regiments and teams have mascots – why shouldn't we?'

'You mean, like a goat or something?' asked Edward.

'Yes – but where can we get a goat?'

'My father keeps pigeons,' said Ricky. 'But I don't think he'd lend us one for a mascot. Besides, it would only keep flying home again. That's their instinct.'

'I've got a pet tortoise,' said Edward. No one spoke. 'Well . . . it was just an idea.'

'I know!' Fen exclaimed. 'What about our cat? It would be a great mascot.'

'What's he called?' asked Stass.

'It's a she,' said Fen. 'She's called Baskerville.'

They all laughed.

'Baskerville!' said Ricky. 'That's a dog. Sherlock Holmes – "The Hound of the Baskervilles".'

'I know that,' said Fen. 'My parents have always kept a lot of dogs. We got her as a stray kitten, so she grew up with dogs. They treated her like another dog, and she behaves like one. In fact, she thinks she *is* a dog!'

'I hope she's not as fierce as the Hound of the Baskervilles,' said Edward, who had read all the Sherlock Holmes stories and wanted to be a detective in his spare time from writing dictionaries.

'No, she only looks fierce,' said Fen. 'She has this wild sticky-out mane of black hair, and bright green eyes.'

'She sounds a perfect mascot,' said Ricky. 'Can you bring her along to the next meeting, and we'll swear her in?'

'She won't have to wear red spectacles, will she?'

'No, I think we'll excuse her the spectacles.'

'When is the next meeting?' asked Stass.

'How about tomorrow?'

'It's Saturday,' said Stass. 'I have to work in the shop in the morning.'

'Will the school be open?' Ricky asked.

'Yes,' said Fen. 'There are always matches or drilling practices on Saturdays.'

'Right, let's meet here at two o'clock, then we can have plenty of time to work out our plans.'

'What sort of plans will they be?' asked Edward.

'We'll all think some up,' said Ricky. 'As I said, I've got one I'm working on already. To do with the statue of Sir Rumbelow Spencer.'

'And I've got a notion of how we could make great entertainment in Grenthia Sinful's class,' said Fen.

'Tomorrow, then,' said Ricky. 'And meanwhile, remember . . . '

He began the chant, and they all joined in:

'Stamp your feet, nod your head –
Spectacles on, and we all see red!'

5

Getting away next day for the meeting of the new Red Spectacles Gang was not as easy as they had all hoped.

'What are you doing with the cat basket, Fenella?' Fen's mother asked, as she looked at herself in the hall mirror late on Saturday morning. She was wearing a green tartan skirt and long white woollen stockings, a very expensive designer sweater, and a tartan beret with a red bobble on top, set at an angle on her head. This was her latest golf outfit, and she was off to display it in one of the ladies' competitions at the golf club.

Fen had dragged the travelling cat basket out from the pile of jumbled objects in the cupboard under the stairs, and was putting a rug in the bottom of it.

'I was going to take Baskerville for a little outing,' she said.

'Where on earth to?'

'Oh – just to see some friends. We're forming a sort of club and making Baskerville a member.'

'I did hope you would take the dogs for a good long walk this afternoon.'

'I would, but I promised these friends. Baskerville will be our champion.'

'That cat would make a good champion dog, the way it behaves. All right, I'll leave a note for Lionel to take them when he comes back from the match. Bye-bye, darling.'

'Bye, Mama. I hope you get a high score.'

Fen's mother sighed. 'Fenella dear, how many times must I tell you, it's the *low* scores that do best in golf! Well, I must fly. . . . ' She went out.

Fen found Baskerville in the living room, lying asleep on the hearth rug. As she looked at the cat, she had a brilliant idea: Baskerville might not be able to wear red spectacles, but at least she could have a red collar.

Fen went into the back garden, where the three dogs were sitting or lying on the paved patio. They jumped up when they saw her, wagging and snuffling.

'Sorry, dogs, no walks just now,' she said, petting one of them – a sleek red setter. 'Now, Hercules,' she said, 'you won't mind if Baskerville borrows your collar, will you?'

Hercules didn't mind, but Baskerville was not so keen. It was only after much coaxing and petting, and producing several of the dog biscuits Baskerville loved, that Fen was able to get the red collar fastened round the cat's neck.

After that, Baskerville decided it was time to go back to sleep. She spat and grizzled when Fen tried to pick her up. Finally Fen laid a trail of dog biscuits across the living-room floor, leading into the hall and ending in the open basket.

The cat followed the trail, munching as she went, and when she got into the basket, Fen closed the lid. There were grunts and protests from inside as Fen eased the basket on to the handlebars of her bike, resting it on the pannier in front.

As she rode weavily down the street, passers-by glanced curiously at the wobbling cyclist with the basket from which came a series of screeching miaows – or were they the yappings of a dog? With Baskerville, it was often hard to tell.

'Stass, you're a good boy, you know that?'

Stass looked up warily from the counter where he was weighing tomatoes for a customer. When his mother gave compliments like that out of the blue, he knew that there was bound to be a request afterwards. He was right.

'I have to do a lot of cooking this afternoon – will you stay on in the shop for a bit?'

Stass had to think quickly. A gang meeting wasn't going to be any kind of excuse, but he thought of something that would.

'Sorry, Mum,' he said, 'but I was asked to go to a meeting at school. We're forming a new . . . a new kind of team.' He glanced in his father's direction. Mr Filipou was a football fanatic, and always encouraged Stass's hopes to get into one of the local junior teams. His father regularly railed against Mr Maddox for only allowing rugby and not soccer to be played at the school.

Stass's scheme worked. His father said: 'A new kind of team? At last that Maddox is going to allow real football!'

Stass didn't actually agree. That would have been lying. On the other hand, he didn't deny it.

His father said: 'Of course he must go to the meeting!'

Edward had a different problem. His mother and father didn't usually bother whether he was around or not – they were too busy having arguments and shouting at each other. Edward spent many hours in the peace of the public library. But today, his mother told him to baby-sit while she went shopping.

'I baby-sat on Wednesday,' he complained.

'Well, you can baby-sit again.'

'But Dad's at home,' said Edward, 'can't he mind Larry?'

'I wouldn't leave *him* in charge of a stuffed canary!' his mother said scornfully.

His father came into the kitchen just then, and said: 'Oh, is that right? Well, if you can't trust me with the brat, how can you trust a kid like Edward? He's daydreaming half the time, when he's not got his nose in some blasted book. He wouldn't notice if the baby fell into the bath and drowned!'

'And *you* wouldn't care if it did!' shouted Edward's mother. 'You never wanted to have him in the first place!'

'Nor did you. Remember? "I'm not going through all that again," you said. "It's bad enough with the pair we've got!"'

'I love that baby!'

'Well, take him with you to the shops then!'

'I'm certainly not leaving him here, with you around!'

As the argument went on, Edward slipped out of the back door. He didn't know whether to be glad or sorry that neither of them seemed to notice.

In the back yard, Ricky looked at his watch. It was half-past twelve. He stood staring at the brick wall at the side of the yard. Beside it stood a bucket, and a brush.

His father put his head out of the pigeon shed.

'Are you all right, Ricky?'

'Fine, Dad, fine.'

'You've just washed that wall, and it's as clean as you'll ever get it. Why are you staring at it?'

'I told you, Dad, it's an experiment. I mixed a special powder to put in the water.'

'Are you inventing detergents now?'

'Just the opposite. If the mixture works, that wall will have green streaks on it when it dries.'

His father smiled and said: 'Well, if watching walls dry is your idea of entertainment, I'll leave you to it.'

He returned to his pigeons. Ricky went on gazing at the wall. He hoped he'd remembered the ingredients for the powder correctly. It was one of those tricks he had been shown by his uncle Mike, who was always doing conjuring shows and inventing things like this powder. His uncle had originally used it to make a kind of invisible ink that showed up green when it dried. Now Mike was in Australia, so Ricky couldn't check the formula with him.

Suddenly, Ricky felt a surge of excitement. There were definite faint green streaks appearing on the wall.

'Dad! Dad!' he called. His father came out of the shed. 'Look!' cried Ricky.

His father peered at the wall and said: 'Yes, it's got a green tinge all right.'

Ricky was grinning widely. 'That'll fix Sir Rumble-Guts!' he said.

His father looked at him suspiciously. 'Ricky, what are you up to?'

'Nothing much, Dad. It's only for a kind of game at school.'

'Well, don't do anything rash – you know what happened at the last place!'

'That was an accident, Dad.'

56

'One of many.'

'I'm accident-prone.'

'I know,' said his father resignedly. 'I just hope Jacinta isn't.'

He looked up at the cloudy sky. He was expecting one of his prize pigeons home, and it was overdue. Ricky looked up too. There was no sign of the bird.

Then he looked at the wall again. It was visibly streaked with green. His uncle Mike would be proud of him. What a shame he couldn't be there to enjoy the fun when the powder worked its magic on Sir Rumbelow Spencer's statue!

When Ricky arrived at the school gates, the others were waiting outside.

'Is the coast clear?' he asked.

'No problem,' said Fen. 'Miss Jellinek is refereeing a lacrosse match over there on the playing field. We can go in and round to the back of the school, and no one will notice.'

'Right, let's go!'

Fen picked up her basket from the ground.

'What's that?' asked Ricky.

'A surprise!' Fen smiled.

Before long, they were inside the boiler house and busy with the opening ritual:

'Stamp your feet, nod your head –
Spectacles on, and we all see red!'

As they ended the chant, each of them held their red spectacles up with a flourish, then put them on.

Ricky said: 'I declare the Red Spectacles Gang is now in session!' The others applauded. 'And first,' Ricky went on, 'I have some good news to report.'

He bent down and reached into his duffel bag. From it he took two jam jars, full of a grey powder. He held them up, one in each hand, saying:

'Behold the magic powder!'

'What does it do?' asked Fen.

'It turns Sir Rumbelow green.'

'The statue!' Fen exclaimed. 'Are you going to put that stuff on it?'

'No,' said Ricky, 'but Kenneth is.'

He explained the plan which they would put into action on Monday when the statue-cleaning began.

'I can't wait to see the Mad Ox's face!' said Stass.

'And Kenneth's!' said Fen. They all laughed.

There was a snuffling sound from the corner of the boiler house.

'What was that?' asked Edward.

'That,' said Fen proudly, 'is the newest member of the Red Spectacles Gang.' She went across to the cat basket, where the snuffling sound had come from, and brought the basket into the centre of the room. She undid the strap that held the lid down.

'I would like you all to meet our gallant mascot – Baskerville!' Fen flung the lid open. They all stared eagerly.

Slowly, the bushy-haired head of the cat was raised above the edge of the basket. Baskerville peered all around with wide eyes, twitching her whiskers. Then she wrinkled up her nose and gave a long-drawn-out sound that was like a cross between a miaow and a dog baying at the moon.

Fen said: 'Come on out, Baskerville, we're all your friends here.' She bent down and lifted the large cat out of the basket. 'Now – let me introduce you. Baskerville, this is Ricky, Stass and Edward.'

'How do you do, Baskerville,' said Ricky solemnly, holding out his hand. To his surprise, Baskerville raised her right paw. He took it and gave it a formal shake.

'That was neat!' Stass exclaimed. 'I've been trying to teach our dog to do that for ages.'

Suddenly Baskerville stiffened, and pricked up her ears.

'She's heard something!' said Fen. They all listened.

Outside the door, in the yard, there was a scrabbling sound. Then they heard a metallic scrape, as if one of the dustbins was being moved.

'There's someone out there,' whispered Stass.

'We must keep quiet – they won't know we're in here,' said Ricky.

The scrabbling and scraping continued. Then they heard a soft thud on the door. And another.

'Someone's trying to get in,' said Fen. 'Look at Baskerville.'

The cat was crouched on the top of the basket, staring at the door. Then she gave a long, slow growl. There was silence from outside the door. Suddenly, Baskerville leapt off the basket and landed just in front of the door, giving out a series of yapping sounds. From the other side of the door there came several answering barks.

Fen laughed. 'It's only a dog!'

'Let's open the door and see what happens,' said Ricky.

'Right!' said Fen. She was sure Baskerville was well able to cope with any other creature. She took hold of the handle and pulled the door open. There outside was a terrier. It stood still, gazing with surprise at the scene before it. Baskerville had

59

arched her back and was staring at the dog, her fur sticking out all over her.

The dog thought cats were meant for chasing; it gave a loud snarl, then opened its mouth and snapped at Baskerville's nose. The cat drew back its head just in time to avoid being bitten. Then to the surprise of everyone, including the dog, she jumped high into the air, and landed on the terrier's back, digging in her claws.

The dog gave a yowl of pain and began rushing around in circles. Baskerville clung on. The dog shook itself as it rushed about, panicking. It was like watching a rider on a bucking bronco in a Wild West show.

Finally, the dog ran for the gate that led out of the yard, and as it did so, Baskerville jumped off its back and landed on top of one of the dustbins. The cat had a look of satisfied triumph as she watched the dog go yelping away.

'Nice work, Baskerville!' said Fen, and they all cheered and clapped. The cat got down from the bin and walked slowly back into the boiler house. There she climbed on top of the basket, lay down and went to sleep.

'What a performance!' said Ricky. 'That is the most amazing cat I have ever seen.'

'Stunning!' said Stass. Fen smiled with pride.

'I've just realized something,' said Edward suddenly.

'What's that?' asked Ricky.

'Do you know who I think that dog belongs to?'

'Who?'

'The Mad Ox!'

'Really?'

'Yes. After all, his house is only over there, the

far side of the playing field, isn't it? I saw him with a dog on a lead once, walking along the road. I'm sure it was just like that.'

'No wonder Baskerville took an instant dislike to it,' said Fen. 'And I've just realized something else. I reckon it's that dog that's been messing up the rubbish. Mr Grimley told me the Mad Ox is threatening to fire him because of the mess. Suppose it was his own dog, all the time!'

'If we can prove that, what a victory for the Red Spectacles Gang,' said Ricky. 'But first of all, here's to victory on Monday, when Sir Rumbelow turns green!'

'I would like to thank all those who put their names down to help with the cleaning of Sir Rumbelow Spencer's statue,' said Mr Maddox at assembly next morning. 'It shows commendable school spirit. I have selected the first six names on the list, and the cleaning team will be led by Kenneth Johnson. Their work will commence at the morning break. I am allowing them to miss the following lesson in order to complete the task.'

Ricky looked at Kenneth, sitting two rows in front. He was looking around him with a self-satisfied smile. Ricky smiled too, as he thought what the Mad Ox's reaction was likely to be, later in the day.

At the break, Kenneth was bossing his team of statue-cleaners around.

'Simon and Caroline, you fill the buckets. John, fetch the cleaning liquid. Harry and Martina, we'll need two step-ladders, one each side of the statue.'

When everything was ready, Kenneth picked up a scrubbing brush.

'Hold the ladder steady, Simon,' he said. 'I shall now climb up and make the first scrub at Sir Rumbelow's head.'

There were two buckets standing beside Kenneth's ladder, and two by the ladder at the other side. Ricky was among the group of onlookers standing around near Kenneth's ladder; Fen was beside the other ladder.

Ricky said: 'You'll need to do a lot of scrubbing up there, Kenneth – there's been a few pigeons on the old bloke's head.'

'There'll be more than a pigeon on *your* head if you don't watch out, Speccy Four-Eyes!' said Kenneth. Suddenly, he threw the scrubbing brush straight at Ricky's upturned face and said: 'Oops, sorry.'

Ricky stepped back just in time. The brush hit the ground with a thud, just in front of him. Angrily, Ricky picked it up and was just about to hurl it at Kenneth, when the rasping voice of Mrs Froom cut through the air:

'Stop! Redman, what are you doing?'

Ricky said innocently: 'Kenneth dropped his brush, Mrs Froom. I was just going to hand it back to him.'

'Were you, indeed?' Mrs Froom stood silent for a few seconds, beaming her laser eyes on Ricky. Nobody moved. Then she said: 'If you had learned to have a bit more school spirit, you'd be helping with the cleaning, instead of standing around gawping. You will write out a hundred times: I MUST BE A DOER, NOT A WATCHER, and bring the lines to me tomorrow morning.'

'Yes, Mrs Froom,' said Ricky. So far he had been given lines as a punishment by Miss Grenfell and by Mrs Froom in his first week. The new school was certainly giving him a lot of writing practice.

'Very well. Now climb the ladder and give the brush back to Kenneth.'

Ricky climbed up and handed the brush over. Kenneth stared down at him with a triumphant smile on his face. Ricky twisted his own face into a hideous grin, then stuck his tongue out. He climbed down the ladder.

'That's better,' said Mrs Froom. 'Now, carry on cleaning!' She turned and strode away towards the school.

The bell shrilled for the end of break. The plan had been delayed, and it was now or never. Ricky looked across at Fen and pointed up in the air. He had been going to give the shout himself, but now people would just think he was trying to cause further trouble. Fen would have to do it.

She understood the signal. She raised her arm and pointed to the sky, calling out: 'Look out, Kenneth, a pigeon!'

'Where?' asked Kenneth. He looked up, and so did everyone else. As the crowd gazed up, Ricky and Fen each shook the powder from their jars into the buckets, then hid the empty jars in their pockets.

'There's no pigeon, you twit!' said Kenneth.

'Sorry – my mistake,' said Fen, smiling. 'Well, must rush!' She and Ricky followed the rest of the pupils who were hurrying into the school building. On the steps, they looked back with a smile at Kenneth and his team dipping the cloths and brushes in the buckets and climbing up the ladders, giving the stern figure of Sir Rumbelow a thorough washing.

6

It was the second lesson after the break, and Kenneth and his cronies had come in just after the start, to draw attention to themselves. Miss Grenfell congratulated them on their cleaning of the statue, and Kenneth smiled around, altogether too pleased with himself.

Miss Grenfell began telling them the history of Fuddlecombe Manor.

'You will be able to see the actual sword which Lord Jasper Fuddlecombe wielded when he rode into battle with the Charge of the Light Brigade.'

'Wasn't that one of the greatest disasters in military history, miss?' asked Edward eagerly.

'Yes, Edward, as a matter of fact it was,' said Miss Grenfell coolly. 'However, it was extremely gallant.'

'And what about the ghost, miss?' said Edward.

'Ghost? What ghost?'

'The ghost of the headless knight, miss. The one who was killed in the Crusades.'

Edward had spent Saturday morning in the library, and discovered a reference to a Fuddlecombe ancestor who had indeed gone off to the Crusades and never returned. He had also read about Tarquin, a nephew of a much later Lord Fuddlecombe, who had indulged in black magic and tried to conjure up spirits. It had caused scandal locally, and Tarquin was hastily sent off to Australia.

Edward had decided that one of the spirits Tarquin tried to conjure up must be the ancient knight, who would undoubtedly have had his head cut off by his enemies. And if Tarquin could conjure him up, why shouldn't the Red Spectacles Gang do the same?

'Well,' said Miss Grenfell, 'I know there was an early ancestor of the Fuddlecombes' who went to the Crusades and never came back, but I don't think I've heard of anyone seeing his ghost.'

'Oh, I read about it in a book, miss. He carries his head in his hands, and wails.'

'Nonsense, Edward. I assure you, you will be seeing no ghosts at Fuddlecombe Manor when we make our tour next week.'

Miss Grenfell went on with her account of the Manor and its former residents, but her most lavish praise was for the current Lord and Lady Fuddlecombe.

'They really are fine people – *wonderful* members of the aristocracy, truly an example to us all. We are *so* privileged to be able to go round their stately home . . .'

'I expect they need the money, miss,' said Ricky.

'I beg your pardon?'

'From the visitors, miss. It's a good idea, really. Helps to pay the bills. I was thinking of suggesting it to my dad.'

'Suggesting what?'

'That we charge for people to come and look round our house. It's very interesting. My dad keeps pigeons in the back yard.'

'That's quite enough from you, Ricky Redman,' said Miss Grenfell. 'I just hope you will know how to behave when you are in Lord Fuddlecombe's house.'

'Oh, I will, miss,' said Ricky earnestly.

'He wouldn't know how to behave in a farmyard,' said Kenneth, and Caroline and Simon laughed.

Just then, the door burst open and Mr Maddox strode in, his hair wild and his moustache twitching.

'Oh, good afternoon, headmaster . . . ' said Miss Grenfell, but Mr Maddox simply grunted and strode up to the platform. He glared around the class ferociously, then stuck out his finger accusingly. He was pointing straight at Kenneth.

'Kenneth Johnson!' he boomed.

Kenneth stood up, open-mouthed. 'Y-y-yes, sir?' he stammered.

'How *dare* you? How *dare* you?' shouted Mr Maddox, looking purple in the face. 'You, of all people! It's an outrage! A crime against humanity! An insult to the school!'

'W-w-what is, sir?' asked Kenneth, frightened and utterly bewildered.

'The statue, boy, the statue!' yelled Mr Maddox. 'You were supposed to wash it, not paint it green!'

'I . . . I don't understand, sir,' said Kenneth.

'Oh, you don't, don't you?' snarled Mr Maddox. 'Then come outside and look at your handiwork. And the rest of you!' He strode to Kenneth and took hold of his left ear between his thumb and forefinger. Kenneth winced as the headmaster led him out towards the door.

Caroline and Simon followed, looking at each other with puzzled and very alarmed expressions. The whole of the rest of the class began to push and jostle to follow on behind. Miss Grenfell flapped her arms up and down, saying, 'Don't rush! Don't rush!'

Outside, Mr Maddox was standing, still holding Kenneth's ear, in front of the statue of Sir Rumbelow Spencer. With his other hand he was pointing up at the figure of the school's founder.

'Look at it! Look at it!' he screeched.

They all looked up. The bulky stone figure was streaked with a hideous green colour: the long Victorian coat, the trousers, the top hat which Sir Rumbelow was holding in the crook of his arm, all looked as though some giant snail had crawled all over them, leaving broad slime-trails of green in its wake.

As for the head, with its moustache and abundant side whiskers and grim, staring expression – one eye looked as if it had a green eye-patch across it, the whiskers were mottled, and the face looked as if it had been attacked by some particularly horrible form of green acne.

There was a hush of horrified fascination in the gazing group below. Ricky let his eyes flicker from one face to another. Kenneth's mouth was open in disbelief, and he was swallowing hard. Caroline's eyes were blinking at a great rate. Even Simon's usually wooden-looking face was twitching.

Mr Maddox was frowning like thunder at the sight before him and breathing heavily, puffing his cheeks in and out. Ricky caught Stass's eye, and winked.

Mr Maddox broke the silence.

'WELL?' he roared. 'What have you got to say for yourselves?'

'I . . . I don't understand it, sir. It was absolutely clean when we finished.'

'Absolutely clean,' echoed Caroline, tearfully.

'There must have been something in the water, sir,' said Kenneth.

'Something in the water!' the headmaster snorted. 'You are either knaves or nincompoops! And whichever you are, you're to stay after school today and clean that foul green colour off that statue, if it takes you all night!'

'Yes, sir – we will, sir,' said Kenneth, cringing.

After school, Ricky saw Kenneth standing at the door of the school caretaker's room, pleading with Mr Grimley.

'But we must have it, Mr Grimley, *please*! The really strong detergent, the stuff that cleans drains and all that. I'm sure it's the only thing that will get the stain off.'

'You shouldn't have put it on in the first place,' Mr Grimley growled.

'I didn't,' said Kenneth. 'Not the green. It's some kind of trick, and when I find who did it, I'm going to pulverize him into pulp!'

'All right, all right,' said Mr Grimley, who clearly disliked Kenneth. He produced a large bottle. 'You can have this. Mix it with some water, and don't get it on your hands and face. Better wear gloves when you use it.'

'I haven't got any gloves here,' Kenneth whined. 'Except my cricket gloves, of course.'

'Then wear those.' Mr Grimley shut the door.

Ricky wandered out and stood on the steps at the entrance, watching Kenneth and his team prepare to clean the statue again. Fen came out, and so did Stass and then Edward.

'Personally, I think Sir Rumbelow looks better green,' said Ricky.

The others agreed.

Ricky said: 'Let's meet for a conference at head-quarters in five minutes. We'll move off and go separately, so as not to attract attention.'

As Ricky went past the group at the statue, he looked at Kenneth putting on his cricket gloves, and said: 'Be careful batting against Sir Rumbelow, Kenneth. He's a demon bowler.'

Kenneth scowled. 'If you had anything to do with this, Redman,' he said, 'I'll beat you to a jelly, then have you thrown out of Spencer's like you were out of the last place!'

'Now, now, no temper tantrums, Kenneth,' said Ricky. 'Sir Rumble-Guts is watching you.'

In the boiler house, after the chant and the spectacles ceremony, they congratulated each other on the success of their plan for the greening of Sir Rumbelow.

'I thought the Mad Ox was going to explode!' said Stass.

'And did you see Kenneth's face, looking at the statue?' said Fen.

'Did you see Sir Rumbelow's face?' said Ricky. They all laughed, and did imitations of Sir Rumbelow's expression.

'At last we're having a bit of fun at this boring old school!' Fen exclaimed.

'Thanks to the Red Spectacles Gang!' cried Stass. They all took off their spectacles and raised them in the air, like a salute.

Fen had an idea. 'Maybe we should use some of your powder to paint this place a bit,' said Fen. 'It could do with brightening up.'

'Yes, and we could decorate the boiler with paintings – like they had in caves and old hiding places,' said Ricky.

'We could do hieroglyphics,' said Edward, 'like the Egyptians. Then no one else would know what they meant. It would be our special code.'

'Great,' said Ricky. 'Why don't you work some out, Edward? We could do with some better chairs too, that don't keep falling to bits.'

'And even a carpet,' said Fen.

'We'd need some money for those kinds of things,' said Stass, 'and I'm broke.'

'Who isn't?' said Edward.

'I know how we could get some money,' said Ricky.

'How?' asked the others.

Ricky took the three oranges out of his duffel bag and began to juggle with them.

'Busking!' he said.

'Like the people who do shows in the street?' asked Stass.

'That's right. They just leave a hat on the pavement, and if the show's any good, people stop and watch, and put money in it.'

'Well, you're fine with your juggling, Ricky,' said Edward. 'But what could the rest of us do?'

Ricky stopped juggling and looked around at them thoughtfully. 'I know!' he said. 'Stass is a great dancer. He could do that.'

'Sure I will, if you like,' said Stass eagerly. 'I've been inventing this new kind of dance. It's sort of a combination of Greek dancing and tap dance.'

He hummed a tune and did some fast, clattering steps. The others began to clap in rhythm, and soon Stass was whirling around the room, his feet kicking and tapping and sliding, and his arms swaying. He stopped and made an exaggerated bow. There was loud applause.

'Wonderful, Stass,' said Ricky. 'We'll call you Stass the Stepper.'

'Thanks,' said Stass. 'It would be even better if we had some proper music, though.'

Fen said hesitantly: 'Well . . . maybe . . . '

'What is it, Fen?' Ricky asked.

'Well, I found an old banjo not long ago, in the loft at home – it must have belonged to my older brother once. I brought it down, and got a book, and I've been trying to learn it.'

'Perfect!' said Stass.

'But I don't know if I can play well enough.'

'I'm sure you will. The rhythm's the main thing.'

'We'll soon have a proper busking troupe,' said Ricky. 'I've got a few more juggling tricks I'll work on. After school tomorrow, we'll meet here for a practise session.'

'What will you do, Edward?' asked Fen.

'I've been thinking,' said Edward seriously. 'I did wonder about making up a quiz, from my Dictionary . . . '

'Good for a TV show,' said Ricky. 'But not quite right for the street.'

'Then what about a ghost story?' said Edward. 'I could tell my tale of the headless knight of Fuddlecombe Manor.'

'Is there really a ghost there, do you think?' asked Stass.

'Well, there might be,' said Edward. He told them what he had read about the Crusading ancestor, and about Tarquin and the scandal.

They all agreed they didn't believe in ghosts, but none of them sounded very convincing.

'I was thinking,' said Edward. 'Supposing we make sure there *is* a ghost at Fuddlecombe Manor, the day we make the school visit?'

'You can't just ring up and hire a ghost,' said Fen.

'But we could "hire" one of *us* to be the ghost!' said Ricky.

'That's right,' said Edward. 'And the others could do the spooky noises and sound effects.'

They talked eagerly about the plan to conjure up the ghost of Fuddlecombe Manor. They needed to know the layout of the house, and where the tour would go, so Ricky and Fen agreed to tag on to one of the public tours the following Saturday and see how the scheme could work best.

'That was a great idea, Edward,' said Ricky.

'Do you think I could be a ghost for the busking too?' Edward asked eagerly.

'It wouldn't be too easy, out of doors,' said Fen.

'Then maybe I could be a comedian, and tell a few jokes?'

The others looked doubtful, but Edward went on: 'My father is always telling jokes he hears in the pub. My mother hates it, but I overhear him telling them to my uncle. I don't understand all of them, but maybe the audience would.'

'And maybe they would think a young fellow like you ought not to know that sort of joke at all!' said Stass.

'Well, what about all the jokes that go around in school?'

'Adults don't seem to like us telling those, either,' said Ricky. 'See if your father has any good, clean jokes.'

'I'll ask him,' said Edward.

73

'Same time tomorrow, then,' said Ricky. He began the chant, and they all joined in. Then all of them but Ricky put their spectacles carefully away.

Ricky went towards the door. He opened it, then quickly closed it again and turned to the others with his finger to his lips.

'What's up?' whispered Fen.

'Mr Grimley's coming – he's dumping some rubbish sacks in the yard.'

'Did he see you?'

'No, I don't think so. We need a spyhole in this door so we can see what's going on outside. Just until we get closed-circuit television, of course!'

'There's a bit of a crack just here,' said Stass, pointing to a spot near the bottom of the door.

'Great!' Ricky knelt down, and got a penknife out of his pocket. He scraped away at the crack, peeling off some splinters of the wood. Then he put his eye to the slit.

'What can you see?' asked Stass.

'Mr Grimley's dumped the black sacks against the wall. Now he's going over to a sack on the ground. It seems to have split. He's starting to pick up some of the spilt rubbish.'

'We're trapped here till he goes, I suppose,' said Fen.

'We need a secret entrance – a tunnel or something,' said Edward.

'Like the prisoner-of-war movies,' said Stass.

'*Achtung*! *Achtung*! This is Herr Maddox, Governor of Stalag Camp Spencer,' said Fen, giving a Heil-Hitler salute.

'Talk of the devil! There he is,' said Ricky.

'Who?' asked Fen.

'The Mad Ox. He's come through the gate into the yard. He's calling Mr Grimley over.'

'Let's have a look,' said Fen. She knelt down and peered through the spyhole. 'The Mad Ox looks angry.'

'I've never seen him look anything else,' said Edward.

'Angrier than usual,' Fen said. 'He's waving his arms around.'

'Let's try and hear what they're saying,' said Ricky. He put his ear near the hinge side of the door. Edward and Stass put their ears to the door too. They could hear only the occasional word.

'Disgusting! . . . It's a disgrace!' Mr Maddox was saying.

Mr Grimley's mumbled replies were too low to make out, but clearly the headmaster was blaming him for the state of the yard. Then they heard Mr Maddox say:

'You're fired!'

There were mumbled protests from Mr Grimley, and they could just hear him saying: ' . . . not my fault.'

'Nonsense!' shouted Mr Maddox. 'Of course it is. Well – I warned you! I'm dismissing you, Grimley. It's one month's notice, from today. Then – OUT YOU GO!'

Fen said: 'The Mad Ox has walked off. Mr Grimley's just standing there, looking round the yard. He seems to be muttering to himself.'

'He's got plenty to mutter about,' said Ricky.

'We can't let him be fired, when it's not his fault,' said Fen. 'We've got to help him.'

'Let's tell him about the dog, then he can explain to the Mad Ox,' said Stass.

'The Mad Ox would never believe him,' said Ricky. 'It would only make him even angrier. We've got to catch the dog red-handed, and prove it's the culprit.'

'That could be tricky,' said Edward.

Ricky said: 'Yes, but no job is too tricky for. . . .' He paused, took off his spectacles, and held them up.

They all did the same, and shouted together: 'The Red Spectacles Gang!'

When Ricky got home, his father was out the back with the pigeons as usual. Ricky went out into the yard. He grinned when he saw the streaks on the wall where he had tried out the powder which had turned Sir Rumbelow green. He patted the wall with satisfaction.

His father came out of the shed, and said: 'Hello, Ricky. Did the powder work?'

'Oh, brilliantly, Dad!'

'Good,' said his father, who was not anxious to enquire too closely just what Ricky had used it for, as long as it hadn't brought down the teachers' rage on him. 'By the way, Ricky, there's a postcard for you. It's in the kitchen.'

Ricky looked at his father, who glanced away. Then he knew the card must be from his mother – and that his father must have read it. He didn't blame him: she never wrote to *him*, and it was too much of a temptation to write on open cards, as she always did. Ricky thought she probably meant his father to read the cards too.

This one was much the same as usual: hoping he was well, saying she was getting on all right, and she missed him, and hoped to arrange to see him soon. She always said that, but the promised meeting had never come about.

The card was sent from the town a hundred miles away where his mother had gone to live when she had run off with the Singing Computer Salesman. Ricky called him that because his mother had met him at some amateur song contest in a pub.

Ricky had been upstairs, and heard the row she and his father had, just before she walked out. It was like the other rows, only fiercer. She accused his father of having no go in him, of not liking to have any fun, of spending all his time with his pigeons or his vegetables. She was going off with someone who had a bit of life in him, she said.

His father protested, said she was being unfair, that he'd always done his best for her. Ricky wished he would shout back and stamp around a bit. But his mild attempts to reason with Ricky's mother only seemed to make her more angry.

Finally his father said: 'What about Ricky?'

'I'll send for him, when I'm settled.'

'He's staying here – this is his home,' said his father.

'It won't be much of a home with just you here!'

'We'll see what *he* thinks about it!'

Ricky knew what he thought about it. He stayed with his father. He was fond of his mother – she was lively and laughed and joked and sang, and told funny anecdotes about the neighbours and the people she worked with at the office. But she was out a lot, and Ricky had got used to being on his own. Sometimes he missed her, and felt lonely, though he would never admit it. He could stand on his own and fend for himself. He certainly didn't want to go off to some unknown town and live with the Singing Computer Salesman.

When his mother hugged him and said a tearful goodbye and promised it wouldn't be for long, he said he would be all right.

'I'll send for you soon. You'll be able to come and see how you like your other home.'

Ricky had kissed her, and smiled. He felt the promised invitation wouldn't come for a long time, if ever – which was just as well, because Ricky planned to make his own life, staying exactly where he was.

As Ricky stood looking at the card, his father came into the kitchen and began washing his hands at the sink. He glanced over his shoulder and said:

'How is she?'

Ricky shrugged. 'There's nothing new.'

'She's not asked you to go there?'

'No.'

His father turned back to the sink. Ricky felt a wave of affection for him. He said: 'Anyway, I'd rather stay here.'

His father began to dry his hands on a paper towel. He nodded and said: 'Good. Good.'

As they started to get a meal ready, Ricky wondered to himself what he would like his father to do. Go storming off to the other town, perhaps, have it out with the Singing Computer Salesman, and drag his mother back. Or at least try to. But it would be no joy for anyone to have them both in the house again and still quarrelling.

And for his father to do that anyway, he would have to change his whole character and way of going on. Was it possible for people to change like that? Maybe his father didn't want to change.

It was strange how grown-up people seemed often to make a mess of their lives, whereas at their age they ought to be able to control what happened to them.

Ricky was determined to control his own life. Just as he controlled the oranges and the other things he juggled with. After the meal, he would go to his room and practise some more tricks, ready for the first rehearsal of the Red Spectacles Busking Gang.

7

At assembly next morning, there was news of a show of an even more exciting kind. Mr Maddox announced that a documentary television film was going to be made, in a series called *Schools in the Picture*. Spencer's was to feature in one of the programmes.

'It is a matter of great pride that our school has been chosen,' said the head. 'What's more, it is a tribute to the firm, disciplined style of education we have established. You will be pleased to hear that the director of this film is none other than an old boy of Spencer's School, and I am going to introduce him to you now. Boys and girls: Mr Harold Harbison!'

There was loud applause in the hall.

On to the stage walked a tall man with untidy black hair, and a big face with a long chin. He was wearing jeans and a roll-necked cream sweater, with a brown leather jacket on top.

He went to the lectern and gripped it firmly, as Mr Maddox stood aside.

'Thank you, thank you!' said Harold Harbison. He held up his hand. The applause died down.

'Now, as the head has told you, I am an old boy of Spencer's – though I like to think not *too* old!' He smiled and paused, expecting laughter. There were some dutiful giggles, from Kenneth and his friends especially.

'We are indeed making a film about the school, and you will all be in it!'

There was clapping and some cheers.

'I can't promise you each a starring role, of course, but we shall be reflecting every aspect of life at Spencer's, and we shall want to hear from you, as well as from the teaching staff, just what the school means to you.'

'If I told them that on the telly, they'd have to bleep it out,' said Fen quietly to Ricky beside her. Ricky grinned.

'They wouldn't bleep out the banjo, though,' he said.

Fen looked stunned. 'You don't seriously think they'd let me . . . ?'

'Why not?' said Ricky. 'They want to reflect every aspect of life here – so we'll give them the Red Spectacles Busking Gang!'

Caroline turned round from the row in front and said loudly: 'Ssssh!'

Fen made a face at her.

' . . . the next week or two,' Harold Harbison was saying, 'you will see me and one or two colleagues prowling about the school a bit, sitting in on classes, watching the sports, hanging about the playground – just observing in general, to decide what we would like to film. Then soon after that, our unit will be here in force, with all our cameras and paraphernalia, to film you all in action. And a month after that, when the programme is broadcast, we shall be showing Spencer's to the nation!'

He held up his hands. Mr Maddox began clapping loudly, and everyone in the hall joined in. Harold Harbison smiled and bowed, basking in the applause. Then he shook hands with Mr Maddox and strode off stage.

Mr Maddox addressed the school earnestly and at length, using words like *unparalleled opportunity*, *putting our best face forward* and *beaming the spirit of Spencer's on to the screens of the nation*.

He wound up: 'Undoubtedly one of the key sequences in the programme will be that activity for which this school is renowned. I refer to our precision marching displays. In the ensuing weeks, we shall have to practise, practise, practise; and I want the entire school to assemble on the playing field for drilling, immediately you've had your lunch. Group yourselves into classes, and we shall decide who will be in the drilling teams to support our top squad in the film. You can look on it as what in the media business would be called an audition.'

In the playground at the morning break, the members of the Red Spectacles Gang gathered in their usual corner.

'We're going to have to practise, practise, practise, too,' said Ricky, 'if we're going to get the busking act into the film.'

'Do you really think he'd put us on?' asked Stass.

'Of course. And when they spot how talented we are, we'll be on TV all the time, and we can say goodbye to this place for good!'

'If only we could,' said Fen. 'I'm afraid he might be more interested in the Mad Ox's marching displays. That's what he'd think was the star attraction of Spencer's.'

'We'll have to think of a way of making sure we get on.'

'What about Baskerville?'

'How do you mean?'

'Everyone likes seeing animals on the telly,' said Fen. 'If we put Baskerville in the busking act, they'd be bound to use it.'

'Brilliant,' said Ricky.

After lunch, the Red Spectacles Gang joined the general drift in the direction of the playing field. They could see their class gathering. Kenneth was already barking orders to Caroline and Simon and one or two others, and they were marching up and down.

'Left, right, left, right, left, right. . . . SQUAD . . . on the march, ABOUT . . . TURN!'

The group of marchers made the turn, stamping their feet, and moved back in the other direction.

As Ricky and his friends watched them, Kenneth called out: 'I bet you lot can't march like this!'

'Stass can,' said Ricky. 'Take it away, Stass!'

He began clapping in time with Kenneth's *left-right* calls, and Stass started to do his leaping dance.

'Ridiculous!' said Kenneth.

Ricky winked at Stass and motioned him to stop. Then he said: 'You're right, Kenneth – we'll help you do it *your* way.'

'Glad you've got some discipline at last,' said Kenneth. He went on calling: 'Left, right, left, right . . . '

Ricky, quietly at first, and then louder, also started saying: 'Left, right, left, right . . . ' except that his timing was the opposite of Kenneth's – when Kenneth was saying *left*, Ricky was saying *right*.

The marchers, confused, began faltering and

stumbling and getting out of step, until finally Kenneth shouted: 'SQUAD . . . HALT!'

The group stopped. Kenneth said: 'I've had enough of your messing, Redman!' He clenched his fists. Ricky stood his ground.

Just then a voice nearby said: 'Your class will have to do better than that, Kenneth!' It was Mr Farmer, who had just arrived on the scene. Kenneth glowered at Ricky, and dropped his arms to his side.

'Right,' said Mr Farmer, 'I'll take charge of this class now. Get in four lines, ready for inspection by Mr Maddox.'

As the Red Spectacles Gang lined up in the back row, Ricky looked across the playing field. Each class had its space on the field, with a teacher in charge. The teachers were getting their groups into some kind of order, with varying degrees of success. Their voices could be heard pleading, urging, or commanding . . .

'Barry Morris, let go of Jane's hair at once!'

'You should have gone, before you came out here!'

'Jonathan, will you *please* stop picking your nose!'

'No, Delia, you *can't* take off your shoes! You'll just have to put up with them squeaking.'

Then the booming voice of Mr Maddox drowned out all other sounds as he spoke into a microphone from the top of the steps of the cricket pavilion, his words blaring from loudspeakers in the pavilion roof:

'Silence! Our marching audition is about to commence. School . . . atten . . . SHUN!'

'That means feet together, Redman,' said Mr Farmer, seeing Ricky standing in a lounging, relaxed posture and taking no notice of the head-master's orders.

'Yes, sir. Sorry, sir. I didn't hear what Mr Maddox said.'

'You didn't *hear*? Good heavens, boy, you must have thick ears as well as. . . . ' Mr Farmer tailed off, remembering what difficulties he'd had when he last referred to Ricky's spectacles.

'As well as what, sir?' asked Ricky innocently.

'As well as . . . thick feet!' Mr Farmer recovered.

'Oh, they're not all that thick, sir . . . ' Ricky began, but the booming voice came again:

'NO CHATTERING IN THE RANKS!' shouted Mr Maddox.

There was silence on the playing field. 'Now, I want all teachers to start drilling their groups, with the commands of *march*, *halt*, *at ease*, *attention*, and *left* and *right turn*. I shall move around amongst you, noting the names of the best marchers, who will be in the squads for our display on television.'

Mr Farmer smoothed back his hair, straightened his tie, and put his shoulders back in what he must have thought was a striking military posture. Then he said in his most mellow tones:

'Very well now, 5A. I'll put you through your paces. Don't let the school down, will you?'

Ricky whispered to Stass: 'No – we'll send it up!'

Stass laughed, and seeing Mr Farmer glare at him, turned the laugh into a prolonged fit of coughing.

'You'd make a fine soldier, I must say, boy!' said Mr Farmer sarcastically. 'As soon as drill starts, you go sick at once.'

Kenneth and his friends sniggered.

'I'm all right now, sir,' said Stass.

'I'm glad to hear it. Now, squad – marching on the spot: Mark time! Left, right, left, right! Pick up those feet, you lot at the back . . . '

The drilling continued. It wasn't long before Mr Maddox came to their group. He stood watching them critically. With him was Mrs Froom, carrying a pen and a large notebook. Ricky thought she looked like the commandant of a prison camp.

Mr Maddox stared with a frown at Kenneth, who was drilling with fierce enthusiasm, stamping hard and raising his knees as high as he could as he marched on the spot.

Ricky whispered: 'If Kenneth lifts his knees any higher he'll hit his chin and knock himself out.'

Stass laughed, and once again covered it with a cough. Fen leaned over from her place in the back row and said: 'Have a mint, Stass.' She held out a packet. Beside her, Edward groped in his pocket for his liquorice allsorts to offer to Stass too.

Then they heard Mr Maddox's voice booming: 'What's going on there at the back? SQUAD . . . HALT!'

Everyone stopped and looked round as Mr Maddox moved purposefully around the group to the back row, Mrs Froom marching behind him.

'I have never seen such a sloppy lot of marchers as this back row in all my born days!' rasped Mr Maddox. 'Scruffy, that's what they are. What are they, Mrs Froom?'

'Scruffy, headmaster. Definitely scruffy,' said Mrs Froom with contempt.

'Do you hear that, you lot?' asked Mr Maddox. 'Now, what are you?'

'Scruffy, sir,' muttered a few of the back row.

'Louder!'

'Scruffy, sir!' they all yelled.

'Certainly not star drilling material!' said Mr Maddox. 'We can eliminate all this row, for a start. So – back row, FALL OUT!'

Ricky fell flat on the ground at Mr Maddox's feet. The head stepped back, startled, and snapped: 'What are you doing, boy?'

Ricky looked up innocently. 'What you said, sir.'

'You ninny!' said Mr Maddox. 'I said *fall out*, not fall down!'

'Sorry, sir,' said Ricky, scrambling up.

Mr Maddox sighed and moved round to the front of the group again. 'Now here we have better drilling potential,' he said. 'Kenneth Johnson, because of your keenness and school spirit, I have decided to forget the statue episode and retain you for the leading drilling squad, together with . . . '

He called out the names of Caroline and Simon and Kenneth's other supporters in the front row, who all said: 'Thank you, sir,' in simpering tones. Mrs Froom wrote the names down in her notebook, and then they both moved on to examine the next group.

Kenneth looked over at Ricky with a sneer.

'You've got no discipline, that's your problem,' he said.

'And you'll have no feet left, if you go on marching like that!' Ricky replied.

The sixty names for the drilling squads in the film display were announced at next morning's assembly.

'I have no doubt,' said Mr Maddox, 'that their performance in the film will bring honour and glory to the illustrious name of Spencer's School!'

There was loud clapping. Ricky saw Kenneth looking around him and smiling with self-satisfaction.

'We've got to take him down a peg,' said Ricky. 'If he's on the telly strutting about in that march, he'll be so puffed up with pride afterwards, he'll be a bigger bully than ever.'

'It's a job for the Red Spectacles Gang!' said Fen.

Mr Maddox was booming from the platform about another kind of job.

'Operation Clean-Up is what we need here at Spencer's. When the eyes of the nation are upon us, we want no shred of litter or unsightly rubbish to defile the shining vision of our noble school. So every day, after school, one class will be detailed to do litter patrol, picking up every scrap of paper and refuse, scrubbing the steps, cleaning the gates and railings, and generally making the whole place spick and span. Class 5A will begin the work today, and you will collect your rubbish sacks and cleaning materials from the caretaker's office immediately school ends.'

Fen looked at Ricky. Class 5A was their class, and they had been planning to have a meeting of the Red Spectacles Gang immediately after school.

Ricky shrugged, and said: 'We'll just have to make the meeting half an hour later.'

'I was going to go home and fetch my banjo, and bring Baskerville back too, so she could join the busking practice,' Fen said.

'That's fine, then,' said Ricky. 'You can go while the rest of us are doing litter patrol. If anyone notices, I'll say you weren't feeling well.'

After school, Mr Maddox was standing beside the

caretaker's door, supervising the handing out of black sacks. Ricky heard him say with quiet menace to Mr Grimley: 'You're to collect them up at the end and bring them round to the rubbish yard. And if I find them once more scattered around and spilling all over the place, you'll be leaving today, without the month's notice – and with no pay either!'

'I told you it wasn't my fault,' Mr Grimley pleaded.

Mr Maddox noticed Ricky and said loudly: 'Move along there, move along! One sack between four, and bring them to Mr Grimley by the main gate. Redman, you can do some step-scrubbing, as you seem to have an inclination to fall down on the ground!'

'Yes, sir,' Ricky said, taking the scrubbing brush Mr Grimley handed him. Stass was given a bucket, and Edward a cake of heavy-duty soap.

'And if I catch you slacking, Redman,' said Mr Maddox, 'I shall give you detention after school for a week. I'm watching you, remember. We all know how you had to leave your last school – and if there's any trouble, I shan't hesitate to tell you to leave this one!'

Mr Maddox turned and strode away towards his study.

'Better get on with it, son,' said Mr Grimley. 'When he talks about kicking people out, he means it!'

'Yes,' said Ricky quietly. 'We heard what he said to you.'

'There's no secrets around here, is there?' said the caretaker bitterly.

'I think we can help you,' whispered Ricky.

'Help me? How?'

'We think we know who's messing up the yard.'

'Who? Tell me, and I'll have his guts for garters!'

'We'll have to prove it first,' said Ricky. 'But we will – somehow.'

'Who's "we"?'

Ricky smiled and, pointing to his glasses, whispered: 'The Red Spectacles Gang!'

When the litter patrol was finished and they had cleaned the steps, they waited for Mr Grimley to take all the black sacks round to the rubbish yard. Then Ricky, Stass and Edward crept into the yard and across to the boiler house.

Fen arrived soon afterwards, carrying an instrument case in one hand and the cat basket in the other.

She put it down, saying: 'Phew! You're quite a weight, Baskerville.'

'It's all those dog biscuits you give her,' said Stass.

'Well, she'll deserve a lot more when she's performing in the busking show.'

She opened the lid of the basket. Baskerville jumped out and began prowling around the boiler house, sniffing.

'What will she do in the show?' Edward asked.

'She could do the shaking-hands trick; and here's another one – watch.' Fen called out: 'Baskerville! Come here, Baskerville!' The cat took no notice, and continued prowling.

'She's not very obedient,' said Stass.

'She's independent,' said Fen, going across and picking Baskerville up. The cat looked up and licked her face.

'Good girl,' said Fen. She put Baskerville down in the middle of the room. 'They teach dogs to do this, but I bet you've never seen a cat do it. Now, Baskerville – PLAY DEAD!'

Baskerville put her head up and gave a long-drawn-out yowl, then dropped to the floor, rolled over with her legs in the air, and lay still.

'Wonderful!' said Ricky, as they all laughed and applauded.

'Well done, Baskerville,' said Fen, giving her a biscuit. The cat sat up again, and munched happily.

'She can walk on her hind legs too – sometimes,' Fen went on. 'But she needs something to reach for.'

'Perhaps this would do,' said Edward. He put his hand in his pocket. They all expected him to bring out the sticky liquorice allsort packet, but instead he produced a small yo-yo.

He began to drop it up and down on its string, and as it moved it lit up and made a whirring sound.

'That's neat,' said Stass.

They all looked at the little sparkling wheel, admiring Edward's control of it. Then they noticed that Baskerville was gazing at it too.

'Baskerville is impressed,' said Fen.

'So am I,' said Ricky, as Edward started doing roll-over movements with the yo-yo, and flicking it up into the air and drawing it back.

Baskerville was getting quite excited. She gave a series of yapping sounds, her eyes fixed on the sparkling object as it gyrated to and fro. Edward moved a step or two backwards, still manipulating the yo-yo.

'Look!' cried Fen.

To everyone's delight, Baskerville stood up on her hind legs, waving her front paws in the air, and began to walk across towards Edward and the hypnotic yo-yo. He backed slowly away again, and Baskerville followed. Then he moved backwards in a circle, and Baskerville turned with him, still standing up, front paws out.

Suddenly, the cat leapt forward and gave the yo-yo a smack with its right paw. It did the same with the left, and then tried the right again. Edward drew the yo-yo up its string, and Baskerville missed and overbalanced, falling down to the ground. Edward stopped the yo-yo and held it out for Baskerville to sniff. The cat put her nose to it warily, sniffed it, and looked puzzled.

Fen knelt down and gave the cat a hug. 'You were brilliant, Baskerville!' The cat wagged its tail, and Fen handed her a dog biscuit.

'That's Baskerville's big trick for the busking act,' said Ricky. '*And* yours, Edward. You're a star with the yo-yo. You should have told us before.'

'I didn't think it would be interesting,' said Edward. 'I'm glad you like it. I did learn some jokes, too. An Englishman, an Irishman and a Scotsman were shipwrecked on a desert island—'

'Better stick to the yo-yo, Edward,' said Ricky quickly. 'Now, I've got the three oranges sorted out, and I'm working on balancing a stick on my chin, with a plate on the end. I'll have to get a plastic plate, though – I broke two before I came out this morning.'

'Well, I've been working on the dance,' said Stass. 'It should be good, with music. Get out the banjo, Fen.'

Fen opened her music case and took out her

banjo. She sat on one of the rickety chairs, and held the instrument on her knee.

'I'm not all that good,' she said.

'Have a go,' said Stass.

Fen strummed the strings, nervously at first. Then she began to pick out some chords, and finally launched into the famous old banjo tune 'Oh Susannah!'

As she played the fast rhythms, Stass began to do his dance, sliding and tapping and leaping. Ricky and Edward started to clap in time. Then Baskerville decided to join in, with a yapping that almost seemed to keep time with the tune.

After a few minutes, Ricky suddenly held up his hand and said: 'Hold on!'

They all stopped.

'Listen!' Ricky said. Outside, they heard the sound of barking.

'The Mad Ox's terrier wants to join in too!' said Ricky.

'We're not having *him* in the act,' said Fen.

'Certainly not! But this could be our chance to prove it's not Mr Grimley who's messing up the yard.'

8

'What's your plan, Ricky?' asked Edward.

'It's simple, really – but first we've got to catch that dog.'

Cautiously they opened the door a little way. The dog, hearing no further noise, had stopped barking and was busy tearing at the rubbish sacks which he had pulled out of the bins. Paper and cans were littered around the yard, and the dog's nose was smeared with baked-bean sauce.

Fen held on to Baskerville.

Ricky said: 'Fen, throw a couple of dog biscuits just out there. When the dog comes over to snaffle them up, I'll sneak out and go round behind him. When you see me wave, open the door wide, so he'll see Baskerville. Keep hold of her. When he sees her, he'll turn and run, and I'll grab him.'

'OK,' said Fen. 'Here goes.'

She threw two biscuits out of the door. The terrier didn't see them at first, but then Stass put his fingers in his mouth and gave a sharp whistle. The dog looked up, and began to come in the direction of the boiler house. On the way, it saw the biscuits, and stopped. Wagging its tail, it picked one up and began eating it.

Ricky slipped out of the door and moved round the side of the yard, unnoticed by the terrier. He moved across till he was between the dog and the entrance to the yard. Then he waved.

Stass pushed the boiler house door wide open,

and Fen crouched down, holding Baskerville firmly. The cat glared at the terrier and began spitting and snarling. The dog looked up in alarm. When it saw its enemy, it gave a yowl of fear, turned and ran for the gate.

Ricky dived forward and grabbed it round the neck. It wriggled and squirmed and snapped, but Ricky got a firm grip on its collar and kept behind it, kneeling down on the ground. Stass rushed over to help him hold on to the dog.

'Quiet, boy, quiet!' said Ricky. Then he called: 'Give him a biscuit.'

Fen handed Edward the packet. 'I'll put Baskerville in her basket,' she said, 'and come and give you a hand.'

She took the cat back inside the boiler house, while Edward came over towards the dog, looking very wary.

Stass said: 'Hurry up, Edward. Give him a biscuit.'

Fearfully, Edward held one out. The dog snatched it and started crunching savagely. Edward looked at his fingers, just to check they were all still there. He plucked up courage and held out another biscuit, then another. The dog calmed down and munched away, giving the occasional growl. Fen came to join them.

'Here's my plan,' said Ricky. 'We'll empty out one of the rubbish sacks and tuck it through his collar, and knot it there. Then we'll tear a hole in it, and put it round his neck like a sort of ruff. He won't be able to get it off.'

Fen said: 'Then whoever sees him will know he's been at the rubbish?'

'That's right. There'll be no one about in the

school now, except for the Mad Ox. He always stays late and writes out timetables and marching plans and stuff. And with any luck, Mr Grimley won't have left yet. Come on.'

'But we don't want the Mad Ox to see us,' said Stass. 'He'll think it's a put-up job.'

'He won't see us at all, if my plan works.'

They tore the sack as Ricky had said, and fixed it to the collar. The dog looked as though it was wearing some kind of ill-fitting black skirt that was stuck round its neck and trailing behind it. But it couldn't get at the sack to tear it off – and in any case, it was greedy for the biscuits Edward kept holding out.

'Now, Fen and Edward,' said Ricky. 'You lead the way out of the yard, and keep giving biscuits to the dog. Stass and I will hold on to its collar.'

Then the strange little procession made its way among the spilt rubbish and the torn sacks that littered the yard, out through the gate, and slowly round to the front of the school. They met no one.

Finally they were all assembled in a group at the top of the main steps, in front of the big closed door.

'What do we do now?' asked Edward. 'I'm soon going to run out of biscuits.'

'We'll push the dog in through the door, into the main hallway. Mr Grimley's room opens on to it. He'll soon spot the dog and see the sack tangled round its collar.'

'Here goes then,' said Edward, gripping the door handle. He opened the door just wide enough, and Ricky and Stass pushed the dog through it. Edward shut the door. They listened, but everything was quiet.

Then Ricky said: 'I know – we can just look in

through this window at the side, if we stand on tiptoe.' They moved to the window and held the ledge, to raise themselves up a bit. They could make out the hallway inside.

The dog was sniffing around, occasionally twisting its head to try to tear at the sack. But it was tied too firmly to its collar.

'What if no one sees him?' asked Edward.

'We'll have to attract their attention,' said Ricky. 'Fen, can you make a noise like Baskerville, if we open the door just a bit?'

'I'll try.'

They crept back to the door again. Ricky opened it just a little, and Fen put her face into the gap.

She began to imitate the miaows and snarls and snaps of Baskerville. The terrier looked at the door in dismay, then began barking loudly and backing away.

'OK, close the door,' said Ricky. Edward did so.

They all went back to the window. They could see the dog standing in the middle of the hall, barking in the direction of the door.

Soon, the door of the caretaker's room opened, and Mr Grimley came out.

'What's all this?' they could just hear him say. 'What are *you* doing here, you mangy cur? Hey, what's that round your neck? Hell's bells! A piece of sack. It was you all the time, messing up my yard!'

He made a move towards the dog, which had now turned to face him. The dog stood its ground and began snarling, its teeth bared.

'You got me fired, you did!' snapped Mr Grimley. 'But now I've caught you. I don't know how you got in here, but you're not going out again till I've dealt with you.'

The terrier started to bark ferociously. Mr Grimley backed into his room, and came out immediately with a broom. He held it out in front of him, keeping the dog at bay.

Suddenly Mr Maddox emerged from one of the corridors that led into the hallway.

'What's going on?' he shouted above the din.

Mr Grimley said: 'Take a look!'

Mr Maddox looked at the dog, then cried: 'It's Basil! What are you doing here, boy?'

He went across to the dog and held its collar, patting it on the head. Basil whimpered and wagged his tail.

'What do you mean by attacking him?' said Mr Maddox.

The caretaker growled: 'Attacking him? What are you talking about? He'd have savaged me if I hadn't got this broom in my hand!'

'He wouldn't do that, he's a good dog, aren't you, Basil?'

'Then what do you think that piece of sack is doing round his neck? Eh? Eh?'

'What do you mean?'

'I mean, *he's* the one who's been strewing sacks and rubbish all around the yard!'

'Nonsense!' said the headmaster.

'But look at the sack! Where do you think he got that stuck to him?'

'I've no idea.'

'Right then, let's take him round to the yard, and see what he does. If he starts messing around with the sacks, we'll know he's the one.'

'Very well,' said the head angrily, 'and when I've

proved he's not to blame, Grimley, out you go, AT ONCE!'

They glared at each other, then began to move towards the door, Mr Maddox holding Basil's collar. At any moment, the eavesdroppers would be found out!

'Quick!' said Ricky. 'We'll run round the back ahead of them, and hide.'

They sprinted away, rounding the corner of the building just in time. A second later, and they would have been spotted. Before long they were inside the boiler house, and Ricky was kneeling down looking through the spyhole. Fen lifted Baskerville out of her basket.

'That was close!' said Edward. They were all out of breath.

'What do you see, Ricky?' asked Stass.

'They're just coming into the yard now. Mr Maddox is carrying Basil. He's staggering a bit.'

'I'm not surprised,' said Stass. 'That dog's a heavyweight – and vicious with it.'

Ricky said: 'They're looking around at all the rubbish on the ground. The Mad Ox is huffing and puffing. Mr Grimley is pointing at the dog. He wants him to let him go.'

'That will show him!' said Fen.

'The Mad Ox let go of Basil. Get busy, Bazzy!'

They could hear excited barking, and the sound of Basil scrabbling and snuffling at the sacks as he happily tore them apart, scattering yet more rubbish around the yard.

Ricky said: 'Bazz is having a great old time! He must think he's been brought here on purpose to rip up the rubbish sacks.'

'What's the Mad Ox doing?' Stass asked.

'He's really fuming. He's stamping his feet up and down and shaking his fists in the air, and shouting.'

Indeed, they could all hear the rasping voice of Mr Maddox, booming out.

'Basil!' he was yelling. '*Basil*! Come here! Bad boy! Come here at once! BASIL!'

'Is Basil taking any notice?' asked Fen, grinning.

'Not a bit,' said Ricky. 'Take a look.'

Fen put down Baskerville, who promptly put her nose to the hinge of the door, as if trying to see through. The cat was making a sort of thoughtful rumbling noise, and its ears were pricked up, listening to the rumpus outside.

'Basil is having the time of his life with the rubbish,' said Fen. 'And Mr Grimley is standing watching. Now he's saying something to the Mad Ox.'

Mr Maddox's reply was loud and furious enough for them to hear.

'All right, all right, Grimley!' he shouted. 'I admit you're not to blame. And I take back what I said about firing you. But I want you to put a heavy padlock on that gate. It's no wonder a dog can get in, the way it is now. Basil, come here I say!'

The members of the Red Spectacles Gang looked at each other. They were all worried, and all thinking the same thing: if the gate to the yard was going to be padlocked, how were they going to get to their headquarters?

Meanwhile, they were trapped inside the boiler house, unable to get away until the headmaster and Mr Grimley had left the yard.

It could be a long wait, thought Ricky, as he looked through the spyhole in the door. Mr Grimley and the Mad Ox were chasing round the yard, trying to catch Basil. They kept tripping over the sacks and their contents, which were strewn all around.

Finally they cornered the dog, and Mr Maddox grabbed his collar.

'Bazzy, you're a very bad boy,' he said.

'I can think of stronger words!' said Mr Grimley.

'Well, keep them to yourself!' growled Mr Maddox. 'And find me a piece of rope or some kind of lead.'

Grumpily, Mr Grimley scrabbled around in the rubbish and found a length of twine. Mr Maddox tied it to Basil's collar and began leading the dog out of the yard.

'What about all this lot?' Mr Grimley called after him.

'You'll just have to clear it up,' said Mr Maddox. 'You've proved your point. Now get the place locked up properly.' He dragged Basil out of the gate.

Mr Grimley looked round the yard. He seemed to gaze for quite a time in the direction of the boiler house. Then he began putting the scattered rubbish back into sacks. The gang stayed still. They were afraid the slightest sound would expose their hide-out. Once or twice, Baskerville began to purr loudly. Fen stroked her and whispered 'Ssssh!' in her ear.

Ricky peered through the spyhole. Mr Grimley hadn't heard anything. But then Edward suddenly started gasping and drawing in his breath, trying to stifle a sneeze. They all looked at him fearfully.

Ricky swiftly took off his anorak, and just as Edward sneezed loudly, he flung the anorak over his head. It muffled the sneeze but it still sounded loud enough inside the room.

Fen knelt down and looked through the spyhole. She saw Mr Grimley raise his head and listen. She held her breath. Then she saw him shrug, and go on filling a sack.

'It's OK,' she whispered.

'I'm sorry,' said Edward miserably, his head emerging from the anorak. Fen gave him a mint. He thanked her and put it in his mouth, adding a couple of liquorice allsorts for good measure. He stood there and chewed steadily, his cheeks bulging.

'You look like a puff adder, Edward,' said Stass, grinning.

'It's better than letting him sneeze,' said Ricky.

Finally, Mr Grimley finished his clearing up, and left the yard. Breathing a sigh of relief, they quietly opened the door of the boiler house.

'What will we do when he puts a lock on the gate?' asked Stass.

'Learn to pole-vault!' said Ricky cheerfully. The others looked at him in alarm, half believing he meant it . . .

Next day, when everyone was in the playground at the morning break, they saw Mr Maddox appear on the main steps with the director, Harold Harbison, and a young woman.

She had carefully made-up eyes, and blonde hair. She wore neat grey jeans and a smart leather jacket, and had a large red and white striped pen hanging from a lanyard round her neck. She was carrying a clipboard.

The Red Spectacles Gang watched from their corner of the playground.

'The Mad Ox is chattering away like a monkey,' said Fen.

They watched the headmaster nodding and smiling as he talked, occasionally patting Harold Harbison on the back.

'He thinks Harold will give him his own TV series.' said Ricky. '"The Ox on the Box"!'

The headmaster shook hands with the director, then with a final nod and wave, went back into the school building.

Harold Harbison stood on the steps, gazing round the playground. He said something to the young woman, who seized her pen and wrote it down on her clipboard. Then he held his fingers and thumbs together so that they made a rectangle, and held them up to his eyes.

He began to turn, still looking through his finger rectangle as if it was a pair of binoculars. He surveyed one part of the playground, then another.

By now, most of the groups had stopped what they were doing and were staring at the pair on the steps. Kenneth was even combing his hair.

Harold Harbison realized he was the centre of attention. He called out: 'Carry on playing, please, children! We're just doing a recce. Act naturally, and try to ignore us.'

Self-consciously, people took up what they were doing.

'What's a recce?' asked Stass.

'I think it's short for "reconnoitre",' said Edward. 'It means suss it out, do a survey to plan something.'

'Like we're going to do at Fuddlecombe Manor,' said Fen.

'Yes,' said Ricky. 'But meanwhile we must get

103

ourselves noticed by Harold. This could be our big chance.'

'For the busking?' asked Edward.

'Yes,' said Ricky. 'We just want to give him a taste of what we can do, so he'll want to see more and put it in the film.'

'But I haven't got my banjo – or Baskerville!' said Fen.

'A snatch of juggling and a few steps of Stass's dance will do,' said Ricky.

Stass said: 'It looks as if Kenneth and his mob are trying to get into the act too.'

They looked across the playground, where Kenneth was shaking hands and introducing himself to the director. He made a few marching steps on the spot, then came to attention smartly, saluting at the same time.

Harold Harbison looked startled. Then he smiled and nodded, and said something to the young woman, who wrote it down on the clipboard. They began to move away, but Kenneth put his hand on the director's arm, and began talking and smiling and sweeping his hand about.

'I think he's offering to show Harold around,' said Edward.

'Or even offering to direct the picture,' said Fen.

'Whichever it is, Harold's getting a bit fed up with him, I'd say,' said Ricky. 'Let's go!'

He pulled the oranges out of his duffel bag, and began juggling with them, throwing them high in the air. The others saw Harold's assistant glance in their direction, then attract the director's attention. He looked across the playground, with Kenneth still jabbering at him.

To Kenneth's annoyance, Harold Harbison

nodded curtly to him and made his way across the playground, followed by the young woman. He stood a few metres away from Ricky, looking through his fingers.

'Do a few steps, Stass,' said Ricky. Stass did some of his dance routine.

'Well, well,' said Harold Harbison. He turned to his assistant. 'Believe me, Fiona, they never taught things like that to us when *I* was at Spencer's!'

Fiona gave a high-pitched laugh rather like a horse's neigh.

'It's part of the manual dexterity course, sir,' said Ricky, stopping his juggling. The rest of the Red Spectacles Gang looked at him in astonishment.

'It's very progressive at Spencer's, sir,' said Ricky. 'We're even encouraged to perform to the public.'

'Really?' said Harold. 'It was all much more rigorous in my day. Jolly fine marching tradition, we had. I hope you modern pupils are still as good. I want you to do your stuff for the cameras.'

'And manual dexterity too, sir!' said Ricky eagerly.

'Yes, good thinking. Show the variety of exercise the school provides. Take down their names, Fiona.'

'Will do, Harold.' Fiona came bustling forward with her clipboard held out.

'We'll finish our recce today, and be back for filming in ten days' time,' said Harold. 'I'm looking forward to getting the old place on film. Labour of love, that's what it is, a labour of love. Know what I mean, Fiona?'

'Oh, yes, Harold. Super!'

Ricky thought Fiona blushed just a little. Perhaps when the director talked about a labour of love, he

105

meant more than just the making of the film. Suddenly he thought of something he must say, to avoid their scheme being nipped in the bud.

'Mr Harbison, sir,' he said, as the director began to move away. Harold Harbison turned back.

'Yes?'

'I wonder, as a favour, sir – would you mind not mentioning to the Mad Ox . . . I mean, to Mr Maddox . . . that you might be filming our manual dexterity demonstration? It would be great if it could be in the film as a sort of surprise for him.'

Harold Harbison chuckled. 'Nice idea, nice idea! A kind of secret tribute, eh?'

'That's right, sir.'

'Secret, of course, until the entire nation sees it on their screens!' He laughed, and Fiona joined in with her high-pitched neigh.

The Red Spectacles Gang all smiled politely.

After school was over, they each made their way round the back to the gate of the rubbish yard. There was a large padlock on it. They stared at it gloomily.

The gate was made of iron, with heavy straight bars close together. Even Baskerville would have found it hard to squeeze between them. The gate, like the brick walls which surrounded the yard, was over two metres high. They all peered in through the bars. Beyond the bins and sacks, they could see the boiler house, which they now felt was a kind of second home, their secret headquarters hide-out.

But what good is a hide-out if you can't go and hide in it?

'Let's go round the side,' said Ricky. They moved

round the corner and along the wall. They looked up. It seemed to tower above them.

Ricky said: 'If I kneel down, one of you could climb on my back. Then I'll stand up, against the wall. You can get up on to my shoulders, and you should be able to reach the top.'

'I'll have a go,' said Stass. Ricky knelt down.

It wasn't long before Stass was up there, standing on his shoulders. 'I can see over the top,' he called down. 'I'll see if I can heave myself up. Stand firm, Ricky!'

Stass gripped the top of the wall, and jumped. Scrabbling with his feet, he was able to clamber up and sit on the top. 'I made it!' he cried. 'Come on up, it's a great view!'

Ricky knelt down again. 'You go next, Fen,' he said.

But Fen held back.

'What's wrong?' asked Ricky.

'When the three of *us* are over, how are *you* going to climb up?'

'Yes, that's a problem. I haven't perfected my pole-vaulting yet. In fact, I haven't even got a pole. We'll have to go back to the drawing board on this one. I've got an idea how we could do it, but I'll need to do a bit of work on it.'

'So we'd better wait till the next meeting,' said Fen.

'I guess so. We'll meet here tomorrow after school, OK? If my scheme works, we'll all be able to get over into the yard. And from now on, we've got to practise, practise, practise, for the busking act. Remember the Red Spectacles Gang are going to be television stars!'

The other three found Ricky's words inspiring:

they each decided to have a practice session on their own at home that very evening. But they found the budding TV star's life is not an easy one . . .

9

Stass decided he needed metal on his shoes, to make the proper tap-dance noises. He got his best black leather shoes out of his cupboard, and hammered several brass drawing pins into the heel and toe of each.

He dragged back the big round carpet from the middle of his room, and stuffed it under the bed. He drew the curtains and switched on the table lamp, turning it so that it lit up the centre of the wooden floor like a spotlight.

He stood in the light, looking down and admiring his shoes. Then he went across and switched on his tape recorder. A blast of lively Greek music came from it.

Stass bowed to an imaginary audience, then began his invented dance, leaping and tapping his feet in a wild, whirling display. The metal on the shoes was a great improvement. It really made a good noise. Perhaps soon he would be able to afford the proper 'taps' professional dancers wore. After all, television dancers must earn a lot of money.

The tune ended, and Stass took a bow, seeming to hear the roars of applause and cheering in his head. The next number began, an even louder and faster one. He launched into another dance, a really frantic one this time.

Soon he seemed to hear more roars of approval from the imaginary crowd. They were cheering in the middle of the dance: this was true success!

Then he realized the roaring wasn't imaginary – and it certainly wasn't approving. It was his father's voice, shouting: 'Anastasios! Anastasios! Stop it! Stop that row! It's like an earthquake up there! STOP IT RIGHT NOW!'

Stass was just going across to switch off the recorder when the door burst open. His father stood there, hands on his hips, his black bushy eyebrows narrowed in a fierce frown.

Stass switched off the machine.

'Sorry, Dad,' he said. 'I was just practising.'

'Practising for what? To be an elephant imitator? Your mother and I are going deaf down there.'

'Yes, deaf!' said his mother, loudly, appearing behind his father in the doorway.

'It's for a show. A gang of us at school are—'

'I told you that school wasn't the right one for him!' cried Stass's father, turning to his mother. 'Look what they teach them!'

'It's not in the classes, Dad,' Stass protested. But he was cut short by a loud scream from his mother. She pointed at his feet.

'Your best shoes!' she wailed. 'You're clumping about in your best shoes! Take them off at once.' Stass hesitated.

'You heard!' said his father. 'Take them off.'

Stass took off his shoes and hastily went over to the cupboard – but his mother said: 'Wait! Let me see them. There's something shiny on the bottom!'

With a sigh, Stass moved slowly across the room, holding out the shoes. There was going to be no more practising tonight.

Edward was trying out his yo-yo in the back yard. It was annoying to have to practise with his five-year-old sister Mary watching him earnestly as she stood beside the baby's pram.

His father and mother had been having a shouting match, and his mother had told Edward to take the other two outside. From here, they could hear the argument still going on. It would die down into silence for a while, now and then, and then start up again.

Edward knew it would end up as usual, with his father stomping out of the house and slamming the door, and his mother using the three of them as an audience for her complaints about their father. He was used to it.

But today he couldn't slip off to the library, he had to keep an eye on the other two. The baby was sleeping through it all, but Mary looked as if she might start bawling at any moment. At least the yo-yo was a distraction.

After a while, Mary reached out her hand and said: 'Give me a go, Edward.'

'In a minute,' said Edward. 'I've got to practise.'

'What for?'

'A show.'

'What sort of show?'

'It's a secret – it's for our gang at school. Mind you, to practise properly, I really need a cat. Maybe you could imitate a cat for me?'

'No – I don't want to.'

'You'd just have to walk after me, pawing at the yo-yo.'

'Why don't you get Rex?'

Rex was the next-door neighbours' Labrador – a sloppy, spoilt dog that expected to be hugged and petted all the time. Edward had never known Rex to obey any command at all, and the idea that he might walk on his hind legs to order was absurd. But Mary had already gone to the low fence that separated the back yards of the houses, and was calling: 'Rex! Rex! Come and play!'

The big, honey-coloured dog got up and ran across to the fence. It jumped and scrambled, and Mary helped it over. She knelt down and cuddled the dog, which squirmed happily and wagged its tail and licked her face with its large tongue.

'I don't think this is such a good idea, Mary,' said Edward.

Mary ignored him. 'Come on, Rex boy, stand up,' she said. She held his front paws and walked backwards a step or two. Rex wagged and licked – he hardly cared what people did, as long as he was the centre of attention.

Mary called over her shoulder: 'Start the yo-yo, Edward!'

Edward didn't want to argue with her just now – it was better to distract her from the argument indoors. Reluctantly, he began flicking the yo-yo about.

'Look, Rex, look!' said Mary. She pushed the dog towards Edward. Delighted to see that someone had produced a new toy to amuse him, the dog made a grab for the yo-yo, which Edward hastily pulled in and clasped in his hand. He backed away.

The dog followed, wagging his tail and barking with glee. Edward slipped and fell to the ground. At once Rex was on top of him, licking his face, then nuzzling and sniffing to find the new toy. Edward tried to push him off, but Rex thought this was part of the game too. He gave a friendly tug at Edward's sweater. The pair of them wrestled frantically on the ground.

'Stop, Rex, stop!' said Edward.

'Is this what your show is like?' asked Mary with interest.

Edward heard the front door of the house slam as his father went out, and soon afterwards his mother came out to the yard.

'Edward, get up at once, and come inside, all of you! I can't leave you on your own for a moment! Rex, get out of it! Go home!'

Rex knew a determined command when he heard one. He retreated over the fence. Edward scrambled to his feet, thinking how performers with animal acts really had a hard time of it.

Fen found herself with the same problem as Stass: noise. She had been practising her banjo in her room for only ten minutes, with Baskerville sitting on the bed beside her and joining in with the occasional yowl, when the door opened.

Her mother stood there, smiling. But Fen knew the smile didn't mean: 'What a lovely sound! Do go on playing!'

Fen stopped and looked up. Her mother came in and sat down on the chair. She leant across towards Fen and spoke earnestly.

'Fen darling, you know how much your father and I love you to have artistic self-expression, and how much we both adore music, but . . . '

'But for God's sake stop that dreadful row!' Fen was smiling. Her father was home on one of his rare breaks from his business journeys abroad. He was downstairs now, probably watching a programme about money on the television.

Fen's mother said: 'Well, those weren't your father's exact words, but the message is right.'

'I've got to practise, Mum – it's for a show some of us are doing.'

'A show?'

'Yes – it's got dancing, and juggling, and yo-yos, and Baskerville is in it, too, doing tricks.'

'Very dangerous, my dear.'

'Oh no, she won't come to any harm, honestly . . .'

'I didn't mean that. I mean there's a danger people won't notice your performance at all – they'll be looking at Baskerville. When I was in the theatre, people always said: "Never act with children or animals – they're bound to steal the show."'

In the past, Fen's mother had been a leading figure in the local amateur dramatic society, and she had once been recruited, with others in the town, to swell the numbers in the chorus of a touring production of 'Hello, Dolly!' But she always said: 'When I was in the theatre' as though she had had her name in lights all over the West End of London.

Fen's mother went on: 'Yes – avoid children and animals, that's what they said. Mind you, I suppose there's nothing *but* children and animals in your show, so maybe it doesn't matter. I think you might have chosen one of the dogs, though – they're much cleverer than Baskerville.'

'No, they're not. Baskerville is the cleverest animal in the entire world. Aren't you, Baskerville?'

Baskerville blinked and twitched her nose.

Fen's mother said: 'I remember once, in "Cinderella", Billy Fitzherbert had the idea of using a real pony to draw Cinderella's coach to the ball. I told him it wasn't a good idea, but he wouldn't listen. Oh no – a real pony it had to be. Well of course, on the first night, what should happen just as they drew up at the steps of the palace? My dear, it was devastating!'

She gave a peal of laughter. 'I said to Billy afterwards, "Manure is all very well in its place, but that place is *not* on the royal doorstep!" Well, of course, the audience was in hoots . . .'

Fen listened patiently. She had heard this story many, many times before, and was happy enough to hear it again, because it was funny and her mother enjoyed telling it. However, it looked as if there would be no banjo practice tonight.

Ricky's father was standing in the back yard, gazing up at the sky. Now and then, he looked at his watch – a high-tech instrument which had a stopwatch and many other features built into it.

When Ricky came out, he began looking up too. They stood in silence for a short while. Then Ricky said: 'Which pigeon are you expecting, Dad?'

'Pippa,' said Ricky's father. 'She should be here within the next half-hour, if she's to make any kind of time.'

'Do you mind if I do some woodwork out here?' Ricky asked.

'No – carry on. Is this another school project like the paint powder?'

'Sort of. I want to make some stilts.'

'Is it for one of those marching displays you told me about? You're going to look a bit odd, marching on stilts!'

'It's not for that, exactly.' But Ricky's father had given him an idea. Suppose he *did* join the march on stilts . . . ? For the moment, though, he needed them for a more urgent reason – to get over the wall of the rubbish yard. His father had a batch of square wooden stakes, each two metres long, leaning up against the pigeon shed. He was planning to take them out to his allotment to make a new frame for his runner beans.

He said Ricky could use two of them, and found him a thick plank he could saw up to make the footholds on the stilts. There would be three footholds on each stilt, so that Ricky could start by balancing on the lower ones, then gradually step to the higher ones, still balancing.

His father found screws and tools, and together they set about making the stilts. Mr Redman glanced up every now and then to see if there was any sign of Pippa. She still hadn't appeared when the stilts were finished.

'I'll hold them while you get on,' said Ricky's father. Ricky was pleased with his enthusiasm. He felt closest to his father when they were doing practical things like this together. He knew his father would have liked him to help him more with the work at the allotment, but Ricky found vegetables very boring – they didn't move or do anything, they just sat there and grew.

His father held the two stilts firm, as if they were the sides of a vertical ladder. Ricky grasped them, as high as he could reach. He put his right foot, then his left, on to the lowest footholds.

'OK, Dad – you can let go.'

Ricky hadn't been on stilts for a couple of years, and those were smaller ones. But his body seemed to remember how to balance. After wobbling and having to step off two or three times, he found he was walking quite confidently on the lowest footholds.

Stepping up to the second pair while still balancing was a tricky operation, but finally he mastered it. Then came the third and highest footholds. His father had to rush and hold the stilts a few times to prevent them toppling. At last, here he was, high above the ground, walking like a giant in seven-league boots.

Now the wall of the rubbish yard would be no problem. Three of them could get over on someone else's shoulders, and he would be the final one, using the stilts. Once on the wall, he could pull them up behind him and bring them over to the other side.

'Well done, Ricky!' said his father. 'It won't be long before you can join the circus!'

Ricky didn't say that this was in fact one of his secret ambitions. He strutted about the yard, while his father looked at him, smiling – between gazing at the sky and checking his watch.

'No sign of her,' said Mr Redman. 'Well, better luck next time, eh?'

Ricky found that from his height on the stilts, he could see over the top of the shed. And there, in the distance, he spotted a dark shape flying towards them. He was sure it was the pigeon coming home.

'There she is, Dad! I can see her!' he called. He raised his right hand to point in the pigeon's direction. The stilt started falling. He grabbed at it, but it was too late. It fell to the ground with a clatter. He gripped the other stilt with both hands, and managed to hold it upright for a second or two, but then he felt himself falling, and had to jump.

He stumbled as he landed, and sprawled out on the ground.

'Ricky, are you all right?' his father asked, rushing across to him.

'Yes, Dad, I'm fine. Look! Look up there!'

Above the shed the pigeon appeared. Pippa landed and perched on the roof. Mr Redman clicked his stopwatch and said: 'It's a good time. Pippa, you're going to be a champion!'

He held out his hands. The pigeon fluttered down towards him, and Ricky picked himself up and went to join in the congratulations.

Ricky carried the stilts to school next morning, and hid them outside the back wall of the rubbish yard. When school was over, the Red Spectacles Gang gathered there.

Stass, Fen and Edward were soon up on the top of the wall, using the shoulder-climbing methods they'd tried before. That left Ricky down on the ground.

He stood two metres away from the wall, holding the stilts upright. He stepped on to the lowest footholds, and steadied himself, moving the stilts with jerky little steps forwards and backwards to keep his balance.

He stepped on to the next footholds, made sure he could balance on those, and then up he went on to the highest footholds. The others saw him sway and wobble for a moment, as if he was going to topple over. Then he steadied himself. Soon he was walking towards the wall.

'Come on, Ricky, you're walking tall!' called Stass.

Ricky reached the wall and made the short jump from the stilts, so that he was sitting beside them. They clapped, and patted him on the back. Stass applauded so wildly that he fell backwards off the wall and landed on all fours.

'Are you all right?' asked Fen. Stass scrambled to his feet and gave the thumbs-up sign.

Ricky pulled up the stilts and handed them over the wall to Stass. Then the rest of them jumped down from the wall. It was a long drop, and Edward hesitated before he made the jump. But although his feet jarred when they hit the ground, he managed to stay upright.

Soon they were all inside the boiler house, chanting:

'Stamp your feet, nod your head –
Spectacles on, and we all see red!'

Edward said: 'I wonder if the ghost of the headless knight wears red spectacles?'

Ricky laughed. 'Maybe we'll be able to tell you after Fen and I do the recce of Fuddlecombe Manor tomorrow.'

'Have you got the entrance fee?' Fen asked Ricky, as they got off the bus at the gates of Fuddlecombe Manor on Saturday morning.

'Yes – my dad was so delighted with Pippa's speed, he was happy to give it to me.'

'My mother gave me mine – she said it was good I was doing something cultural for a change, instead of thinking about clothes all the time. My father was a bit snooty about it: he said stately homes didn't make any profit.'

They walked up to the gates of Fuddlecombe Manor. The main ones were very high and made of black-painted metal with a lot of curls and leafy designs in it. They stood between two fat stone pillars, each with a statue of a swan on top. The swans had a covering of lichen and moss, and the beak of one of them had snapped off.

The main gates were fastened with a chunky metal chain, but there was a narrower gate beside them, opening on to a gravel drive. Inside, there was a booth with a window. They paid their entrance fees and bought a leaflet with diagrams and a history of the Manor.

'The next tour begins in fifteen minutes,' said the woman giving out the tickets bossily, as if she disapproved of children in general and these two in particular.

'Can we just go in and wander about for a bit?' Ricky asked.

'No, you certainly can't!' said the woman. 'You must stay with the guided tour at all times. Go in at the front door and wait with the others in the hallway. And mind you wipe your shoes. Her Ladyship can't bear muddy marks on the marble floor.'

'I bet she doesn't have to clean them off, though,' said Fen softly.

The big oak front door swung open with a long-drawn-out creaking noise.

'That's nice and spooky, for a start,' said Ricky.

They went into the hallway, which had black and white marble squares on the floor. Ricky thought they would make a marvellous chessboard.

There were a dozen or so other visitors waiting, some looking at the family paintings on the walls, two or three sitting on a carved wooden bench. There were other chairs by the walls, but they had silk ropes across them.

'What's the point of having chairs you can't sit on?' said Fen.

'They're posh chairs,' said Ricky. 'Only suitable for the bums of the gentry.'

'Gather round, please, ladies and gentlemen,' said a harsh, teacherish voice. A tall woman in a severe black suit with a high-necked white blouse was standing in the middle of the hall. She was carrying a short stick like a conductor's baton, and tapping it against the palm of her hand.

There were now about twenty visitors in the hall, most of them adults, though there was one child of five or so, who was holding the hand of her mother and yawning a lot.

'Quiet, please!' said the guide in a commanding tone. She waited for silence, then went on: 'Welcome to Fuddlecombe Manor, which has been the home of the Fuddlecombe family for countless generations. Around the walls here you will see some portraits of the ancestors of Lord and Lady Fuddlecombe, who have graciously allowed us to make this little tour today.'

'At a price,' whispered Ricky.

The guide frowned in his direction. He smiled back sweetly.

'We shall commence our tour on the ground floor, in the Waterloo drawing room, so-called after the tapestries which adorn the walls, depicting the famous battle.'

She went across the hall and opened a polished wood door. Once again there was a creak.

'They could do with a little oil on the door hinges,' said Fen.

'The creakier the better,' said Ricky. 'All the more ghostly.'

121

They were in a large room with high, curtained windows and a huge marble fireplace. There was an open hearth with several big logs in it, but the fire was not lit. The guide began explaining the tapestries, which showed faded scenes of soldiers and horses and cannons milling around in contorted confusion.

'It's going to be hard to make a ghost convincing here,' said Fen. 'It's all too light, and there's nowhere to hide.'

'I'm sure we'll find somewhere better later on,' said Ricky.

'What about the costume?'

'We've got to work that out too – that's why we've come on this recce.'

They went on from the drawing room to the dining room, where there was another big fireplace, and a vast table set with cutlery and glasses, and with silver candlesticks along the middle of it. A gleaming chandelier hung from the ceiling.

'I wouldn't mind a quick snack,' said Ricky. 'Shall we ring for the butler, Lady Fenella?'

'By all means, Lord Ricky!' Fen was standing near a silk rope which hung near the fireplace; she knew they had such things in stately homes, to ring bells for the servants. She gave it a pull, but there was no sound – no sound, that is, except the sharp voice of the guide.

'Don't touch that!'

'Sorry,' said Fen.

'Those ropes could easily break – they are very antique,' the guide reprimanded her.

'Not much point in having a butler, if every time you ring for him, the bell rope snaps,' whispered Ricky.

'We shall now move on to the library,' said the guide.

Even the library didn't seem to have much scope for ghostly appearances. Maybe there was a fake bookcase with a sliding panel somewhere, but they'd need a long time to find it. Ricky and Fen began to feel gloomy about the project.

But on the way up the grand staircase to the upper state-rooms, Ricky said: 'Look, that's our ghost!'

He and Fen were at the end of the group straggling up the stairs, and had reached the wide second landing. In the corner stood the figure of a knight in armour, a sword held up in his hand.

'We'd never be able to move in it, even if one of us could get into it,' said Fen.

'We wouldn't need the whole thing, just the head part. We can wear sheets or something for the rest.'

'And put on the headpiece!'

'Hey, even better – we can hold the head out in front: remember, Edward said the legend was about a headless knight!'

'Perfect! But even when we've taken the head off, where shall we make him appear?'

'We'll keep looking.'

'Come on, come on, you children!' called the guide from the top of the stairs. 'Don't dawdle!'

'Coming, miss!' said Fen and Ricky, moving speedily up the stairs.

They found the ideal place for the ghost's appearance, in the very next room. It was the state bedroom, where of course King Charles was once supposed to have slept, and where the noblest visitors always stayed. Now it was used only for show, and the curtains were kept closed. The guide said the

123

priceless fabrics of the counterpane and the curtains that hung round the big four-poster bed would fade if they were exposed to sunlight.

'All we have to do,' said Ricky, 'is turn off the lights, and the room will be dark and spooky enough for any ghost!'

'We must find somewhere for the headless knight to appear from. Let's look around.'

As the guide went into glowing descriptions of the carved bedposts and the hangings, and the rest of the tour party gathered round the bed, Ricky and Fen moved quietly around the panelled walls. They came to an elaborate folding screen with oriental designs of birds and ferns, standing on its own. They moved behind it, and then Fen noticed a small knob on one of the wall panels. She gave it a pull, and a door in the wall opened.

They peered in. It appeared to be a big, empty cupboard, two metres deep.

'Let's go in,' said Ricky.

They went in and closed the door gently. They were in complete darkness.

'This is spooky all right,' said Fen.

'Our ghost could appear from here,' said Ricky, 'but how would we get in without being seen?'

Their eyes were gradually getting used to the dark, and they could now see a thin strip of light where the edge of the door was. Then suddenly Ricky said excitedly: 'Look at the back of the cupboard! There's a strip of light there, too. It must be another door. This isn't a cupboard, it's a secret passageway!'

They went towards the far strip of light, and felt around the flat wooden surface.

'Yes, there's a handle!' cried Fen. 'It's another

door.' She pushed, and the door opened a crack. She saw a large room with painted murals on the walls, and armchairs and sofas and polished tables.

'It must be a private sitting room for the people in the state bedroom,' she said.

'And it will be a private entrance for our ghost: we can get in here, ready to scare the daylights out of the people in the state bedroom!'

'Sssh! There's someone coming in!' Fen whispered.

They heard the voice of the guide saying: 'And here we have the guests' sitting room, with the celebrated murals, depicting scenes from country life . . . '

Fen peered through the crack in the door.

'They're all trooping in from the corridor,' she said. 'I wonder why she didn't bring them through here.'

'There would have been a traffic jam,' said Ricky.

They heard the guide say: 'Over in this corner, we can see a painting of the eighth Lord Fuddlecombe, leading the hunt . . . '

'Now's our chance!' said Fen. She opened the door a bit more, and they both squeezed through and out into the room. The guide and the visitors all had their backs to them, gazing at the mural. Quickly they moved across the room and joined the crowd.

No one had noticed. Ricky and Fen grinned at one another. The recce had been a success. Soon they would hurry to the gang's headquarters to meet Stass and Edward, and plan next week's appearance of the ghost of the headless knight . . .

10

Inside the boiler house, Ricky stood like a general beside the map he had drawn with chalk on the wall. It showed the layout of Fuddlecombe Manor, and he was going through the plans they had made for the headless knight's appearance. As he spoke, he pointed with a stick at the various rooms and stairways and corridors.

Edward was only half listening. He was looking at a leaflet about the Manor which Ricky and Fen had brought back. When Ricky had finished, he said: 'You know, there's something odd about this account of Fuddlecombe. It doesn't say anything about Tarquin and all the fuss there was about his magic and stuff.'

'It's a family scandal, I suppose,' said Fen. 'They don't want the public to know the murky bits.'

'Anyway, our ghost will be better than any of Tarquin's,' said Stass.

'Sure it will,' said Ricky. 'Now, let's recap on the gear we have to bring. Fen and I will each borrow a sheet from home, all of us will bring torches, and Stass is in charge of getting two bottles of tomato sauce for the blood.'

'They'll *all* be seeing red on Thursday!' said Fen.

On the Sunday, Ricky spent a couple of hours helping his father at the allotment. They made the frame for the runner beans, and did a lot of weeding.

'Thanks, Ricky,' said his father. 'I owe you a favour. Is there anything particular you want?'

Mr Redman was very surprised when Ricky said: 'Could I borrow a white sheet, Dad?'

'No, you can't practise your banjo tonight,' Fen's mother told her on Saturday. 'I have people in for bridge.'

'How will I get a chance to learn, Mum, if I don't practise?'

'I've got a golf match tomorrow morning,' said Fen's mother. 'And your father's off on another business trip. You can practise then. But keep the windows closed, or the whole neighbourhood will be complaining.'

'Could I ask you something else, Mum?'

'Ask away.'

'Could I have one of those old white sheets in the cupboard in the bathroom? The ones we stopped using when you got the fancy flowered ones.'

'What do you want it for? A play?'

'Well, sort of. For acting, anyway.'

'Ah, it's a toga for Roman dress, is it? I once played Julius Caesar's wife, you know. I was wonderful.'

She struck a dramatic pose and said:

'The noise of battle hurtled in the air,
Horses did neigh, and dying men did groan;
And ghosts did shriek and squeal about the
    streets . . . '

Fen thought: Shrieks and squeals – we'll have to practise a few of those, for Thursday!

127

In the next few days at school, Harold Harbison and Fiona seemed to pop up everywhere – and wherever they went, the teachers began to behave in the oddest ways.

Miss Grenfell kept patting her hair, and started to walk in a curious, slinky way. But Mr Farmer was even more outrageous. He came into school each day in a different outfit. First he wore a blue blazer and a yellow cravat at his neck, with a diamond pin in it, and carried a shooting stick, which he unfolded and sat on, instead of his chair. When he stood up, though, the point of the stick was stuck in the wood of the platform. Ricky and Stass rushed up to help the teacher pull it out, but it came out with such a rush that it hit Mr Farmer under the chin.

Another time, he came in wearing a black cloak and a large fedora hat, this time carrying a silver-topped cane.

'All he needs is fangs and he could be Count Dracula!' said Ricky.

Whenever he could, Mr Farmer would stop Harold and Fiona and boom at them in his mellowest voice about the need to have people who had 'screen charisma' in the film. He would flash his white smile at the pair of them as he spoke.

It wasn't long before Harold and Fiona could be seen fleeing down corridors whenever they saw Mr Farmer approaching.

Even the nervous music teacher, Miss Jellinek, appeared with her hair done in a new style, instead of in a straggly bun as she usually wore it. And Mrs Froom was even seen to smile once or twice when the director was nearby. Fen said her customary frown was better – the icy smile would be enough to freeze the film in the camera.

Mr Maddox behaved liked a more exaggerated version of himself: his roar was more deafening, his gestures more sweeping, his growl of disapproval more fierce. The only unusual thing was that he sometimes tried to make jokes, at which he chuckled loudly himself – which was just as well, because they were so unfunny or so badly timed that no one else laughed at all.

As for the pupils, they glanced or pointed at Harold and Fiona, and sometimes there were giggles and whisperings too. Kenneth and his group were the only ones who deliberately tried to impress the director with their superiority over the rest of the school. Kenneth would go on and on about how good his marching skills were, and how he would probably be an army general one day.

Ricky was lurking nearby during one of these conversations, pretending to read the notice board. He was excited to hear Harold Harbison say:

'Yes, I was talking to one of the regional TV chappies the other day. Mentioned the big marching sequence I'm planning to film. He said he might do a live insert about the film we're making, and feature it in the local magazine programme.'

'Showing us marching?' asked Kenneth, goggle-eyed.

'Exactly. It would be a good bit of advance publicity for my film, and show the school off well too.'

'Wonderful, sir,' said Kenneth.

'Brill!' said Caroline.

Ricky smiled. A marching sequence on live television – there had to be scope there for some entertaining input by the Red Spectacles Gang!'

Ricky had another idea too. After the busking practice in the boiler house on Tuesday after school, he told the rest of the gang:

'You know I was going to write a new verse for that terrible school song we sing every day? Well, I've done it!'

'Great! Let's hear it, Ricky,' said Fen.

Ricky stood up and produced a crumpled piece of paper from his pocket. He sang:

'Hail, glorious Maddox, our heavenly head –
He feeds us on haddocks and slices of bread.
Though others may think him a funny old fool,
We love Mr Maddox, the head of our school!'

The others laughed and clapped. Then they crowded round Ricky to read the verse and sing together. Fen's voice stood out among the rest, pure and musical.

'They should get Fen to sing it as a solo in the film!' said Stass.

'That's what *I* thought, too,' said Ricky, seriously.

'You can't mean it,' said Fen. 'The Mad Ox would never allow it – and he'd come down on us like a ton of bricks!'

'But supposing the Mad Ox didn't know about it, till it was too late?'

'How could we organize that?' asked Edward.

'By seeing exactly where the microphones are when they film the assembly, and getting near enough to one of them.'

'We'll have a go, anyway,' said Fen enthusiastically.

'We won't be able to do anything about it until

130

the day,' said Ricky. 'Except rehearse the song, of course.'

They sang it through once more, for fun. Fen said: 'Even if we get it into the film without the Mad Ox knowing, won't Harold Harbison cut it out later?'

'We'll have to hope he thinks it's a real verse. After all, he knows the Mad Ox thinks he's the greatest headmaster of all time. He might easily have written a special verse to glorify himself.'

'That's true,' said Fen.

'Now,' said Ricky, 'it's time we had a final rehearsal for the visit to Fuddlecombe Manor tomorrow. Let's get out the sheets.'

Edward got the two folded sheets from under one of the chairs. Stass put one over his head.

'I'll suffocate in here,' he said.

'We'll cut a hole for your head,' said Ricky, producing his penknife.

'That's better,' Stass said, as his head poked through the ragged hole they had cut.

'OK, now I'll climb on your shoulders,' said Ricky, 'and Fen can drape the other sheet over me.'

Fen stood on a chair and arranged the sheet over Ricky's head. 'Now you look like a real tall ghost!' she exclaimed.

'There's only one problem – I can't see where we're going,' said Ricky. 'I'll have to cut two eye-holes in the sheet.'

When that was done, Ricky stretched out his hands so that they just poked out from the sheet. Edward handed him a football he'd brought to substitute for the knight's helmet during rehearsals. He had daubed two eyes and a mouth on it.

'OK, shine the torches!' said Ricky. Fen and

Edward crouched down, beaming their torches at the figure.

'It looks really spooky!' said Edward. 'Shall we do the bloodstains now?'

'Sure,' said Ricky.

Fen and Edward each picked up a bottle of tomato sauce and took the top off. They flicked the bottles at the figure in the sheets. Tomato sauce came flying out in a slurp. They began to rub it into the sheets with their fingers.

'Go easy!' said Stass. 'That's my eye!'

As usual, when the sauce was half gone, it began to stick in the bottle. Fen and Edward had to resort to banging the ends of the bottles with their hands. Soon the sheets were streaked and stained with red.

'What a bloody knight!' said Fen. They laughed.

'Now for the moans and groans,' said Ricky. 'All together now!'

They gave out a weird chorus of ghostly sounds. Basil, the headmaster's dog, who was sniffing at the locked gate of the rubbish yard, pricked up his ears in alarm, then ran away as fast as he could go.

'And now we shall proceed up the stairs,' said the guide at Fuddlecombe Manor. 'Please follow me.'

'Come along, children, and don't touch anything!' said Miss Grenfell, shepherding the fifty pupils from Class 5A and Class 5B. Ricky and the Red Spectacles Gang hung back a little. Miss Grenfell did not notice that four of the group were lagging behind her. She was too busy fussing and telling people to keep their sticky fingers off the walls.

As the rest of the group straggled on up the stairs, the Red Spectacles Gang hung about on the second landing where the knight's armour stood.

'They've all gone into the state bedroom,' said Fen.

'OK, let's go!' said Ricky. 'Hold the body.'

The rest of them held the body of the armour firm, while Ricky took hold of the helmet. He raised the vizor, peered inside and whispered: 'Anybody in there?'

Stass stifled a chuckle. Fen glowered at him.

Ricky pulled the helmet up, but it was stiff. He had to twist and turn it, till finally it came loose and he held it in his hands. They were about to creep up the stairs, when Fen held up her hand, listening.

There were footsteps on the marble floor of the hall below: sharp, high-heeled footsteps.

Ricky motioned them all to stay still. The footsteps stopped.

Then they heard a sharp woman's voice call: 'Julia! I told you to put some flowers on the hall table!'

Ricky knelt down and crept towards the banisters. He looked down. A large lady with her hair dyed a bright copper colour, and wearing a tweed skirt, a pink cardigan and a pearl necklace, was standing in the hall. It must be Lady Fuddlecombe herself!

'Julia!' she called again. 'Where *is* that infernal girl?'

Then, to Ricky's alarm, she looked upwards. He shrank back as he heard her call out:

'Julia! Are you upstairs?'

Ricky whispered to the others: 'Get ready to run.'

Lady Fuddlecombe gave one more shout: 'Julia!' Then she sighed and said: 'I give up. I really don't know what staff are coming to these days.'

133

Then to their relief, the Red Spectacles Gang heard her footsteps clatter out of the hall and die away.

'Let's go!' said Ricky. He put the helmet into his duffel bag. Fen and Stass had bags too, each with a sheet rolled up in it.

They made their way quietly up the stairs. At the top, they could hear the voice of the guide talking about the state bedroom and the time that King Charles slept there. The door was ajar.

'In you go, Edward,' said Ricky. 'And when you hear the first moan from us, off with the lights!' Edward slipped in. The group crowded round the bed didn't notice him. He went across and joined them. Soon he would edge backwards towards the door, ready to flick up the light switch beside it.

Ricky, Fen and Stass crept along the corridor to the door of the sitting room. They went in, and across to the door of the passageway.

It was very dark inside. They switched on their torches. Stass and Ricky got their sheets out and put them over their heads. Fen helped Ricky climb on to Stass's shoulders. Then she got the helmet out of his bag and handed it to him. Ricky held it out in front of him.

Fen positioned herself behind the door, shining two torches on to the helmet. Really, she thought, the ghost of the headless knight looked very convincing.

They listened. The guide was just saying: 'Now, we shall proceed into the corridor, and make our way to the state sitting room next door.'

'Ready?' whispered Fen.

'Ready!' came the muffled voices under the sheets.

They began to make a series of moaning and groaning sounds.

In the room, Edward flicked the light switch off, then moved quickly away from the door to mingle with the group.

'What's happening?' asked Miss Grenfell nervously.

'I can hear moaning!' said Caroline, frightened.

'It must be the ghost! The headless knight!' said Edward.

'I don't believe in g-g-g-ghosts!' said Kenneth in a quaking voice.

'A ghost? Don't be absurd!' snapped the guide. Then she gasped, as the standing screen crashed forward towards them on to the floor, and the door of the passageway swung open. There in the spotlight stood the bloodstained figure, holding its helmeted head out towards them.

'The ghost!' shrieked Edward, and began giving a series of screams of terror. As they had planned, this soon triggered off shouts and screams of panic from the rest of the class. Miss Grenfell joined in with high-pitched screams of her own.

But the loudest scream came from Kenneth, who was crying: 'Keep it away! Keep it away! Mercy! Mercy! Let me out!'

With Kenneth in the lead, everyone made a rush for the door that led out to the corridor, stumbling and pushing and tripping over each other.

'Stop! Stop!' shouted the guide – but even she sounded very nervous.

Fen pulled the door of the passageway shut.

'Quick! Bundle up the sheets,' she said. Just as they had rehearsed it, Ricky handed the helmet to Fen, who put it in her duffel bag. Then Stass and

135

Ricky quickly took off their sheets and stuffed them into their bags.

They slipped out of the door at the back of the passageway and into the state sitting room. No one was there. The tour of this room had been delayed by the sudden appearance of the ghost of the headless knight. They could hear the excited, frightened chatter of the crowd milling about out in the corridor.

Miss Grenfell was calling: 'Be quiet, children! Be quiet, please! There's nothing to be afraid of.' But she didn't sound at all sure.

Ricky went across and opened the door a crack.

'Now's our chance,' he said, and the three of them slipped through into the corridor and mingled with the rest, joining in the chatter.

'It was definitely a ghost,' said Fen.

'The headless knight himself,' said Stass.

'And did you see all the blood? It was gory!' said Ricky with relish.

'I feel faint,' said Caroline.

'It didn't scare *me*!' said Kenneth.

'Then why are you looking so pale?' Ricky asked.

Edward came through the crowd towards them. Ricky whispered: 'Nice work, Edward!'

The voice of the guide roared above the chattering voices: 'SILENCE! Will you all be QUIET!'

Everyone stopped talking.

'Now, I am going to settle this once and for all,' said the guide. 'We shall all go back into the room, and I will open that door in the wall. Then we shall sort this "ghost" out!'

'Do be careful,' said Miss Grenfell timidly.

The guide flung open the door. The room was

136

dark and empty. She reached in and switched on the light. Then she strode in.

Ricky and Fen and Edward, with some of the braver pupils, edged in behind her.

Stass pushed Kenneth, saying: 'Go on, Kenneth. You said you weren't scared!'

'N-n-no, of course I'm not.' Reluctantly he went into the room, and Stass followed. Miss Grenfell came in too, blinking in fear of what she might see.

The guide went to the door in the wall panelling and grasped the handle. She opened the door.

'You see!' she said – with some relief, Ricky thought. 'There is no ghost!'

Cautiously, the pupils moved forward to peer into the cupboard. Fen was among those in front. She took a step over the threshold into the passageway, and looked around. Then she saw it – the clue that might give them all away.

Just behind the door, on the dusty floor, lay a green hairgrip. It was hers. It must have come off when they were busy dismantling the ghost. Fen wondered what to do. Now that they had all seen the passageway was empty, they would soon come crowding in.

Fen gave a sharp cry and knelt down, holding her right ankle.

'What is it?' asked the guide.

'I've hurt my ankle, miss,' said Fen. As she knelt, she quickly reached in behind the door and grabbed the hairgrip. She hid it in her hand, still pretending to rub her ankle.

'Can you walk?'

'Yes, miss.' Fen limped out of the passageway. 'It's better now – I'll be fine.'

As she expected, the crowd of pupils, now full of

curiosity and bold once more, surged into the narrow passageway.

'Come out, come out!' said the guide, but no one took any notice.

Ricky said softly to Fen: 'Are you all right?'

'Sure,' whispered Fen. 'I was only faking. I found this behind the door.' She opened her hand to show the hairgrip.

'Wow, that was close!' said Ricky.

Into the room came the bustling figure of Lady Fuddlecombe.

'What is all this about a ghost?' she asked. 'I heard a terrific rumpus going on up here, and came up to find everyone chattering about a ghost in the passageway!'

'We . . . I mean *they* . . . thought they saw a ghost here,' said the guide.

'Absurd! It must have been a trick of the light.'

'That's what I told them, Your Ladyship.'

'Or some of these mischievous youngsters playing a practical joke.'

Ricky and Fen exchanged glances. Fen held her duffel bag with the helmet in it, very tight.

'Oh, they wouldn't do a thing like that, Your Ladyship,' said Miss Grenfell.

Edward said eagerly: 'Perhaps it was one of those spirits like Tarquin tried to conjure up.'

The guide gasped and looked at Lady Fuddlecombe. She was staring at Edward with a face of fury.

'Tarquin!' she exploded. 'How dare you? You know nothing about it. There is no Tarquin in our family, do you hear?'

Miss Grenfell was wringing her hands. She said

138

cringingly: 'Of course not, Your Ladyship, Edward is making it up.'

'No, I'm not!' said Edward. 'Tarquin did magic, he tried to conjure up spirits, and got sent away . . . '

'That will do, Edward!' pleaded Miss Grenfell. 'I'm frightfully sorry, Your Ladyship, it won't happen again . . . '

'No, it bloody well won't!' shouted Lady Fuddlecombe in a most unladylike way. 'I want you all out, at once. Do you hear? At once! I shall have words with your headmaster about this. Now, go!'

'Line up in an orderly manner,' said Miss Grenfell miserably.

'It's now or never,' whispered Ricky. 'They'll all be trooping downstairs again soon.'

'OK,' said Fen. She and Ricky edged through the crowd, and were soon out in the corridor. No one was around. By now, even the most timid ones had been bold enough to join the rest back in the state bedroom.

'Come on!' said Ricky. They hurried down to the landing.

Fen rummaged in her bag and got the helmet out. Ricky held the suit of armour steady while she put the helmet back on.

'There, Sir Knight, you're as good as new!' she laughed.

'Thanks for the loan of your head,' said Ricky, and they hastened back up the stairs, just as the crowd began coming out of the state bedroom, shepherded by the guide and Miss Grenfell, with Lady Fuddlecombe at the back, shooing them on their way.

As they passed the suit of armour on the stairs,

Ricky looked at it and said: 'Goodbye, mate. It's been nice knowing you.'

11

When the Red Spectacles Gang met in the boiler house after school that afternoon, they went step by step through the events at Fuddlecombe Manor.

'Remember how the helmet shone in the torch-light?'

'Did you see Grenthia Sinful's face? She was as white as a sheet.'

'Whiter than *our* sheets!'

'Yes. They wouldn't do for a whiter-than-white commercial.'

'Oh, how that ghost moaned!' They all started moaning and groaning again, then doubled up with laughter.

Edward said: 'Lady Fuddlecombe didn't like being reminded of old Tarquin, did she?'

'You scored a bull's-eye there, Edward,' said Ricky. 'Tarquin is definitely a skeleton in the family cupboard.'

'Like the headless knight,' said Stass.

'I'd love to hear Lady F bawling out the Mad Ox about it all,' said Fen.

Ricky said: 'I expect we'll hear the Mad Ox doing some bawling at *us*!'

Ricky was right. At assembly next morning, Mr Maddox was frowning like a thundercloud. When the school song had been sung, he launched into a furious attack on the behaviour of Classes 5A and 5B at Fuddlecombe Manor. Miss Grenfell had told him it must have been some trick of the light which made everyone think there was something there. But he was more inclined to believe it was a massive joke, and they had all been in a plot to pretend to see the ghost.

If they *did* think they had seen it, then they were all a lot of silly, overimaginative children. But whether it was a joke or an illusion, they must be taught a lesson. The members of both classes would spend two hours after school, on their hands and knees, weeding the entire playing field.

Even more serious was the fact that deep offence had been caused to Lady Fuddlecombe by one particular boy. Mr Maddox glared round the hall till he spotted Edward, and ordered him to come to his study immediately after assembly.

'But it was in the book, sir, in the library,' said Edward, as he stood in front of Mr Maddox's desk.

Mr Maddox banged the desk with his fist, and tore at his hair with his other hand. 'I don't care if it was in the Bible!' he shouted. 'It is not in Lady Fuddlecombe's history of the Manor!'

'Then it's not telling the truth, sir.'

'Truth! Truth!' snarled the headmaster. 'Who are you to talk about truth? I'll be the judge of what's true and what isn't. That's what schools are for, you little upstart! So the teachers can teach *you* the truth. We don't want you getting any ideas of your own. Is that clear?'

'Yes sir.' Edward knew it was all too clear. Mr Maddox had the power. If you disagreed with him, you didn't do it to his face.

'I sometimes wish we were allowed to cane pupils in this school,' said Mr Maddox. 'Then we'd have a chance of *beating* some truth into you. As it is, you will write out, two hundred times, I MUST NOT LIE TO MY ELDERS AND BETTERS. Now, dismiss!'

As the fifty pupils of 5A and 5B crawled around on the playing field, plucking weeds, Ricky found Kenneth kneeling beside him.

'You had something to do with that ghost business, didn't you?' he said menacingly.

'What are you on about, Kenneth? We all saw it. Though some of us were more scared than others.'

'What is that supposed to mean?'

'Suit yourself.'

'I wasn't scared. I reckon it was all a fake.'

'Then why did you run out of the room screaming?'

Suddenly Kenneth put both hands on Ricky's neck and pushed his head down on to the ground.

'Now you can see the weeds properly, Four-Eyes!' he sneered.

'Get off him!' said Stass, pulling at Kenneth's leg.

'*You* get off!' said Simon, grabbing Stass by the arm. Soon there was a scrum of people wrestling and mauling on the field.

A shrill whistle blew, then Mrs Froom's ice-axe voice was heard slicing through the air:

'STOP THAT AT ONCE!'

The wrestlers stopped still, then began to disentangle themselves.

Mrs Froom stood glaring down at them. 'Any more misbehaviour,' she said, 'and you'll stay here weeding all night!'

'That would be a great scene for the TV film,'

whispered Ricky to Fen. 'Night weeding – a gardening lesson at Spencer's School.'

The days before filming began were busy ones for the Red Spectacles Gang. After school every day they met in their headquarters to rehearse the busking show.

Fen was becoming a really expert banjo player, and Stass's dancing was showy, elegant and very fast. His feet moved so quickly you would almost think you were watching a speeded-up film.

Edward had learnt some good tricks, and his yo-yo was sparkling and whizzing down, up and around. Even Baskerville seemed to feel the general excitement and to be really eager to show off her tricks.

As for Ricky's juggling, he learnt to manage four oranges easily, and his plate-on-a-stick routine was nearly perfect. In rehearsals, he did break a few – and there were some puzzled faces in their various homes. Parents were heard saying things like:

'I thought we used to have six of these.'

or:

'Someone's been jumbling up the plates in this cupboard, I can't find the matching ones half the time.'

Snake-charming was one idea: but no one knew where there were any snakes, and there was general agreement in the gang that Edward's pet tortoise would be no substitute.

Then one day as they were getting over the wall into the yard, Ricky said suddenly: 'The stilts! Why didn't I think of it before?'

'How do you mean?' asked Fen.

'I could use them as part of the busking act.'

'Great!' said Stass. 'You could be like those clowns in the circus, or the people in carnival processions.'

'We could make a clown's costume,' said Fen.

'Or even better,' said Ricky, 'a teacher's costume!'

They laughed. Fen said: 'You mean with a black gown? Yes, we could dye the sheets we used for the ghost.'

'And get one of those black mortarboards they wear on their heads at classy school functions, to impress the parents,' said Edward.

'Where can we get it?' Stass asked.

'We could sort of "borrow" one of the teacher's ones,' said Ricky.

Edward said: 'Yes, they keep them in a cupboard in the staff room, where they hang up their gowns.'

'I could have a false moustache, too,' said Ricky. 'A black one, like the Mad Ox's.'

Fen waited for an evening when the family were all out. She filled the bath and scattered the black powder from the tin of dye into it. She dumped the sheets into the water and knelt down beside the bath, squeezing and pushing them around to let the dye soak in. Then she left them in the bath and went off to her room to do some banjo practice.

An hour later, she went back to the bathroom, picked the sheets out of the water and began to wring them out. Baskerville followed her. Fen bundled up the wet sheets and dumped them on the bathroom stool, then she pulled out the plug. As the water went down, it left a black stain all round the bath. Fen began to scrub at it with a flannel, when she heard a growling sound behind her.

She turned to find that Baskerville was pulling at the edge of the sheets on the stool.

'Stop it, Baskerville!' Fen cried, tugging the sheet. But Baskerville just held on more tightly, delighted at this new game of tug of war. They pulled to and fro, till Fen tripped over the stool and fell down on the floor, tangling herself and Baskerville in the sheets. They rolled around, while more and more black streaks from the damp sheets appeared on the floor and the walls.

At last, Fen got the sheets away from the cat, bundled them up and rushed up to her room, where she draped them over two chairs in front of her electric radiator.

She was about to start cleaning up the bathroom, when she heard the front door open and her mother's voice calling: 'Cooo-eee! I'm home!'

'Hello, Mum,' said Fen, coming quickly down the stairs. 'Shall I make you a cup of tea?'

'That would be super, darling,' said her mother. Fen hoped to keep her mother downstairs for a while, so that she would have time for some tidying up. But then her mother added: 'I'll just nip up to the loo, dear, then I'll come down and tell you all about the evening! I got a grand slam, would you believe?'

'Mum, just a minute . . . ' said Fen – but it was too late: her mother was already going up the stairs.

The explanations were long and confused, and the whole story sounded more and more ridiculous as Fen told it. She felt she was lucky to get away with just cleaning up the mess – if it hadn't been for her mother's joy at getting a grand slam, whatever that was, the punishment might have been a lot harder.

Edward had a stroke of luck in getting a mor
board. He went to the staff room one day to hand
in some extra homework Miss Grenfell had given
him to do. She gave him extra work quite often,
and Edward realized it was really to punish him for
mentioning Tarquin and the family scandal to Lady
Fuddlecombe.

Miss Grenfell was alone in the staff room.
Edward took the exercise book out of his satchel
and handed it to her.

'Thank you, Edward,' she said coldly. Then,
seeing him still hovering, she asked: 'Is there anything else?'

'Not really, miss – it's just that I thought I saw
the television people setting up their cameras in the
playground.'

'Really?' said Miss Grenfell, patting her hair. 'I
thought they weren't starting till Monday.'

As Edward had hoped, she went across to the
window of the staff room, which looked out on to
the playground, and peered out. The door of the
cupboard where the gowns were kept was open.
The hooks were empty, since the gowns were all
being worn, but on the shelf above was a line of
mortarboards.

Edward darted across to the cupboard and grabbed one of them. At the window, Miss Grenfell said:
'I can't see anything.'

'Over on the far side, miss,' said Edward hastily,
fearing that she might turn round at any moment.

He had time to push the mortarboard into his
satchel before Miss Grenfell finally turned and said:
'You must have been mistaken, Edward. There are
no cameras out there.'

'Yes, miss. Sorry, miss.' Edward held the bulging

satchel under his arm, and left the room with his trophy. He told himself that he would return the mortarboard later, so it was only a loan – even if it was a loan that the owner didn't know about.

On Saturday morning, the Red Spectacles Gang met in the boiler house for a full dress rehearsal.

Ricky looked a strange figure as he towered over them on his stilts. He was draped in the sheets, which had dried out in large patches of black and dark grey, like a piebald horse. He had the mortarboard on his head, and had stuck a false bushy black moustache above his upper lip.

Stass was wearing a tracksuit in bright Day-Glo colours of red, yellow and green, and a white baseball cap with GIANTS in big black letters on the peak.

Edward had borrowed an old overcoat of his father's, which hung right down to his feet. He had pinned little flags of many different countries to it, so that he looked like a walking advertisement for the United Nations. He had a bird mask on his head with a jutting orange beak, and red spectacles painted round the eyeholes.

Fen had the most dazzling costume of all. She had got her mother to lend her a black jacket covered in sequins, which sparkled and gleamed in the light, and she wore calf-length boots and an imitation cowboy hat.

Even Baskerville had a frilly lace ruff which Fen had made and fixed round her neck.

They were an extraordinary sight as they moved round in a circle, chanting:

'Stamp your feet, nod your head –

Spectacles on, and we all see red!'

They knew their busking show just *had* to be the hit of the film!

The members of the Red Spectacles Gang arrived very early at the school on the Monday morning. They saw a large blue van with the name of the television company on it, in the playground. Nearby was another van, and several cars. Cables led from the big van through the windows of the school.

Inside the hallway, they met Mr Grimley coming out of his room. 'Hello, you lot,' he said. 'You're here bright and early. Hoping for a star part in the film?'

'Well, you never know,' said Ricky, smiling.

'You deserve it, I reckon,' said the caretaker. 'You're good kids – *I* know that, even if certain other people don't!'

He gave a grin, then went out of the main door, into the playground.

'He must know we fixed it to show up the Mad Ox's dog,' said Fen.

'You don't think he knows about the boiler house?' said Stass.

'No,' said Ricky. 'We cover our tracks too well.' He went across to the door that led into the school hall, and peeped in.

There was a camera set up on the stage, and big lights on tall stands around the hall. A microphone was slung across the hall, high up in the middle, and there were microphones on stage, as well as others on stands along the side aisles.

A voice from a loudspeaker made Ricky start. It said:

'Testing, testing, testing, one-two-three-four-five, Mary had a little lamb, and how's your father?'

Ricky noticed a young man in jeans and an anorak, standing near one of the stand microphones at the side. Then a big, wild-looking man, with a beard and a grubby T-shirt with BATMAN on it, peered round the curtains at the side of the stage.

'OK, Joe, that's fine,' he said.

Mrs Froom came on from the back of the stage. She was wearing a dark grey suit and had clearly had her hair done for the occasion. But she looked just as severe as ever.

She stared with disapproval at the wild man, and said with an icy smile: 'Perhaps you . . . gentlemen would care to join your colleagues for a cup of tea in the headmaster's office, before you begin . . . er . . . shooting, is that the word?'

'Spot on, lady,' said the wild man. 'I could use a cuppa, if you haven't got anything stronger.'

'Not at this time of the morning, certainly,' said Mrs Froom, looking startled.

'OK, come on, Joe!' said the wild man. Joe went up on to the platform and they both followed Mrs Froom backstage.

The hall was empty. Ricky turned and beckoned to the others. They all came in and looked around at the lights and equipment.

'If we stand at the end of that row in the middle on the right,' Ricky said, 'we'll be near that microphone, and Fen can sing the new verse into it.'

The headmaster had decided that all three verses of the school song should be sung for the film, instead of just the two they usually sang in assembly.

'If you wait for the last verse and sing during

that,' said Ricky, 'Harbison won't realize it isn't the right words. I don't suppose they ever sang the whole lot in his day, any more than we do.'

'I'd need to grow two metres to reach that mike, though,' said Fen. 'It's right up on a stand, pointing downwards.'

'I'll soon fix that,' said Ricky. 'Keep a lookout!'

As Stass watched the hallway through a crack in the door, and Fen and Edward kept an eye on the stage too, Ricky darted across to the microphone. Outside, they heard the shrill whistle which signalled the time for the pupils to line up and file into school.

'Hurry, Ricky!' said Fen urgently.

Ricky undid the screw that locked the telescopic stand in place, and lowered the microphone down till it was at head height. Then he locked it again, and moved the stand across till it was near the chair at the end of the row.

He was soon back with the others, and they slipped out of the door and back into the hallway, ready to tag on to the rest of class 5A as they came in.

Caroline had done her hair in a ponytail and tied a bright yellow ribbon to it. Fen gave the ponytail a tug and said: 'DING-DONG! Is anybody home?'

'Shut up!' said Caroline.

'Well, Kenneth,' said Ricky, imitating an American accent, 'How does it feel to be a staaar?'

Kenneth was about to reply when the voice of Mr Maddox roared out above the crowd: 'Quiet please, everyone! I said BE QUIET!'

The hubbub quickly died down into silence.

'Now I want you all to file into the hall in an orderly fashion, without any pushing, shoving or talking. We want to create a good impression of Spencer's for our television friends, don't we?'

'Yeah, man!' said Ricky.

The headmaster frowned. 'Thank you for your enthusiasm, Redman,' he said, 'but I'd rather you saved it for your performance.'

'Oh I will, sir, I will,' said Ricky eagerly. But he was thinking of a very different performance from the one which Mr Maddox had in mind . . .

12

As soon as they got into the hall, the Red Spectacles Gang went quickly across to the row they had selected, and Fen took her place on the end chair, next to the microphone.

There was a rustle of excited whispering in the hall as everyone looked at the lights and the microphones. The cameraman and his assistant came and began to tinker with the camera on stage. The wild-looking sound engineer peered round the curtain. The man called Joe moved down the hall and stood at the back.

Then the teachers filed on to the stage from the back, looking very self-conscious – and with reason. The headmaster had insisted that they all wear their mortarboards as well as their gowns for the filming. They lined up in a row in front of the rank of chairs on the platform.

'Look at the Smarmer!' whispered Stass.

Mr Farmer was looking very gloomy indeed. He was the only one not wearing a mortarboard.

'I wonder where his headgear is,' grinned Ricky, looking at Edward.

'I can't imagine,' said Edward.

'Silence, please!' said Mr Maddox, coming to the lectern. He leant forward earnestly and said: 'As you all know by now, this is a great day for Spencer's School. Today filming begins for the television programme which will really put our school on the map. As you can see from all the lights and the microphones and the camera, and our TV friends who are manning them, we are this morning going to film a typical assembly. So now I am proud to introduce once again the noted director and old boy of Spencer's, Mr Harold Harbison!'

There was applause and cheering as Harold Harbison walked on to the stage, followed by his assistant Fiona, carrying her clipboard. Harold Harbison was wearing a blue blazer which had the school crest on the pocket. The blazer was too small for him, and he bulged out of it in front.

'Thank you, thank you!' he said, holding up his hand for silence. 'This is a proud moment for me too. That is why I decided for our first day of filming to wear my old school blazer, and my old school tie.'

Mr Maddox smiled and held his hands out, clapping, and nodding to the audience to join in. Everyone applauded again.

Harold Harbison explained that they were going to film the morning assembly, including the singing of the school song. So first they were going to have a rehearsal.

He nodded to Mr Maddox to begin. The head grasped the lectern and said in his most booming, dramatic voice: 'Good morning, boys and girls of Spencer's School. We shall start the day as usual with a rendering of our famous school song.'

At the piano, Miss Jellinek pounded out the opening chords, much louder than usual. The wild-haired sound engineer poked his head out from behind the curtain, clutching his headphones to his ears, deafened by the unexpected noise. Then he retired again, as the singing began:

'Hail glorious Spencer's, our school of renown,
The pride of our nation, the jewel in its
   crown . . . '

Ricky whispered to Fen: 'Don't sing the new verse this time, wait until they go for a proper take.'

The school sang the three verses, fumbling the last one as Ricky had predicted. Then they sang them again, for a second rehearsal.

The lights were glaring and hot, and made the inside of the hall look as if it was bathed in bright sunlight.

Harold Harbison said: 'Very good, very good. Now this time we are going to film you, so really put your hearts into it, lads and lasses!'

The cameraman's assistant stepped in front of the camera with a black clapperboard and said: 'Spencer's School, Scene One, Take One.' Then he snapped the hinge shut.

Mr Maddox said his opening words, and then the singing started. Ricky could see the camera moving slowly round, filming the other side of the audience first. He suddenly had an idea.

'Quick, spectacles on!' he whispered urgently. The four of them got their spectacles out and had them on their noses by the time the camera's slow movement reached them. When the camera moved away again, they took the spectacles off.

When the singing reached the third verse, the unfamiliar words were still being fumbled and muttered by the school. Fen leaned close to the microphone beside her, and sang softly and purely into it:

'Hail glorious Maddox, our heavenly head –
He feeds us on haddocks and slices of bread.
Though others may think him a funny old fool,
We love Mr Maddox, the head of our school!'

It was not loud enough for the people nearby to
notice that she was singing something different –
but Ricky knew Fen was so near the mike that it
would be loud and clear on the soundtrack.

They repeated the singing again, and yet again,
so that Harold Harbison could get different camera
angles. Each time the gang saw the camera starting
to point in their direction, they whipped out the red
spectacles and put them on. When Harold Harbison
said: 'Cut!' they took them off again. They didn't
want to be spotted by Mr Maddox. They knew
there was no fear of that during the shooting, since
the headmaster was clearly interested only in his
own performance.

Finally they were told to sit down and relax,
while the camera was set up at the front of the
audience to take shots of the teachers on stage.

The gang watched with amusement as the
teachers began preening themselves – patting hair,
looking in make-up mirrors, straightening ties and
adjusting mortarboards. They saw Mr Maddox
suddenly stride across to Mr Farmer, pointing angrily at the teacher's head. Mr Farmer looked miser-
able as he shrugged his shoulders and tried to tell
the headmaster his mortarboard had mysteriously
disappeared.

'Right! Could you take your places please,
teachers!' called Harold Harbison.

Mr Maddox glared at Mr Farmer, and com-
mandingly pointed his finger towards the side of

the stage. Sadly Mr Farmer moved away into the wings, out of shot.

'Old Farmer the Smarmer really looked fed up,' said Stass, as the gang met after school to discuss the day's events and their future plans.

'He missed his chance of stardom,' said Fen.

'Oh no, he'll get that tomorrow,' said Ricky. 'I asked that Fiona, Harold Harbison's assistant, what was on the schedule. She said they're filming classes – including the Smarmer taking our class for geography.'

'I wonder what he'll wear?' said Fen.

'They're filming a walkabout round the school with the Mad Ox in the afternoon,' said Ricky, 'and after school there's marching practice.'

'That doesn't involve *us*, thank God!' said Stass.

'No, except as observers,' said Ricky. 'We've got to work out a way to mess up the marching display when they do it live for the regional telly programme.'

The Red Spectacles Gang were in the classroom ahead of the others for Mr Farmer's geography class. The room was cluttered with cables and lights. In front of the desks, on the left, was the camera, and in the corner at the back of the classroom the wild-haired engineer was setting up his gear on a desk. His assistant was kneeling on the floor, fixing some cables. No one else had arrived.

'Hello,' said Ricky as they came in.

'Hi there!' said the wild-haired engineer. He produced a hip flask from his pocket and took a swig from it, then went on fiddling with his recording gear.

'We've just got to check some of the classroom equipment,' said Ricky. The engineer nodded.

The gang went across to the large world globe on its stand, on the table in the corner opposite the camera. They grouped themselves around it so they hid it from the sound men – who were taking no notice anyway.

'It unclips at the top and bottom, where the stand grips it,' said Ricky softly. 'Just pull the clips away a bit, and I'll turn it.'

In a few moments, the globe was upside down in its stand, and the Red Spectacles Gang moved casually away and started cleaning the board and straightening the desks. The rest of the film crew came in and began lining up their equipment.

The bell went and the classroom began to fill up. The Red Spectacles Gang took their places at desks in the middle of the class. Mr Harbison strode in, giving instructions to Fiona, who scurried after him, writing things on her clipboard. He went across and conferred with the cameraman.

Kenneth was arguing with Sharon, the snuffly girl who usually sat at a desk in the front row.

'*I* should be in the front row for the film. I'm a prefect.'

'But I always sit here.'

'Well, you can't today. You might sneeze and muck up the recording.'

'I won't sneeze! I won't!' But suddenly Sharon took a deep breath, and let out a huge high-pitched sneeze.

'There!' said Kenneth. Miserably, Sharon moved out of her desk and towards the back of the class. Kenneth sat down and gazed round the room, smugly.

Then Mr Farmer made his entrance. 'Good morning, all!' he boomed as he went to the front of the class and on to the platform.

'Good morning, Mr Farmer!' came the chorus. The class gazed at him in amazement as he stood on the platform, smiling around at everyone.

He had decided to wear a white jacket, the kind you saw people wearing at cocktail parties on verandahs in films about colonial life in the Tropics. With it he wore a crimson bow tie, and over it all, his black gown.

'He's certainly made up for losing his mortarboard,' whispered Ricky to Fen.

'That costume is really quite something!' said Fen.

Harold Harbison seemed to think so too. He had gone over to the teacher and was having a muttered conversation with him. There was clearly an argument going on. They heard Mr Farmer say: 'I insist on wearing it!' and Mr Harbison say: 'No way!'

Harold Harbison was again wearing the old school blazer he had worn yesterday. It gave Fiona an idea. She interrupted the argument to say: 'Harold, I've thought of a way to solve the problem. Why don't you and Mr Farmer swap jackets?'

After some grumbling, Mr Farmer agreed. The blazer looked even tighter on him than on the director.

Mr Farmer frowned and said: 'Very well, class – today, we shall be discussing the trade winds of the world.'

As the lesson, and the filming, began, they watched Farmer the Smarmer bloom in the spotlight, and his voice and manner become even more smarmy than usual.

There was much stopping and starting, and movements of camera position, and discussions between the director and the cameraman. Mr Farmer did a number of diagrams on the board, using exaggerated gestures and many different coloured chalks, as if he was an artist painting a picture.

Then he said: 'Now I want someone to demonstrate the movement of these trade winds on the globe over here.'

Kenneth put up his hand immediately.

'Thank you, Kenneth,' said Mr Farmer. Kenneth moved across to the globe in the corner, and the camera moved forward towards him.

'Now, Kenneth, would you like to show us how the trade winds move across the Pacific Ocean!'

'Certainly, sir!' said Kenneth loudly, turning to the globe. 'They move like this, from America across to. . . . ' He stopped.

'What's the matter, Kenneth?' asked Mr Farmer.

'America's in the wrong place, sir.'

'Don't be ridiculous!'

'And it's upside down, sir!'

'WHAT?' shouted the teacher.

'CUT!' yelled Harold Harbison, even louder.

There was a scene of great confusion as both Mr Farmer and the director strode across the room to the globe and peered at it.

'Whoever heard of a globe with the Antarctic at the top?' rapped Harold Harbison.

'It's a mistake . . . a trick. . . . Someone's been tampering . . . ' Mr Farmer spluttered.

Ricky saw the sound engineer glance in their direction. He realized that he probably remembered the group that had gathered round the globe earlier on. Would he give them away?

To his surprise and relief, the engineer gave a big wink, and turned away.

After school, the Red Spectacles Gang stood beside the sports pavilion, watching the marching practice. Mr Maddox was standing on the steps, with a microphone. It was linked to the loudspeakers on the pavilion roof, which broadcast commentaries on matches and athletics races, and it was also used for giving orders during the marching displays.

The star marching squads Mr Maddox had selected marched up and down, while from the speakers came the barking voice of the headmaster:

'Squad . . . on the march . . . about . . . TURN! Right . . . WHEEL! On the march . . . left . . . TURN!!'

Ricky saw Harold Harbison and Fiona and the cameraman approach. They were discussing and pointing and nodding, as they talked about how to film the marching. They stopped nearby.

'Good afternoon, Mr Harbison,' said Ricky.

'Hello,' said the director.

'I was wondering when you'd be filming the marching display, sir.'

'On Thursday afternoon,' said Mr Harbison. 'I gather you are all to have the afternoon off, in order to stand on the sidelines and cheer.'

'And what about the live broadcast, sir?' That was the one Ricky was interested in.

'Oh, that will be a different crew, from the local TV network. They're bringing in an outside broadcast unit to feed in to the six o'clock news magazine the same evening. We'll have finished our own filming by then.'

'We'll be doing our busking show in the square, sir – you know, the one you said you'd like to film as a surprise for the head?'

'Oh yes, I did, didn't I? What about Saturday morning? Ten o'clock?'

'That's fine.'

Ricky went back to the others. They were delighted with the news of Saturday's performance. Then Ricky said:

'In the meantime, we've got to get ourselves organized for the marching display – and I've got an idea what we can do to mess it up in a spectacular way.'

'But if we get them to mess it up,' said Stass, 'won't they just stop filming and do it again till they get it right?'

'Oh, we won't interfere with Mr Harbison's filming at all,' said Ricky. 'But when he's finished, the local TV people are going to get them to do some more marching, and that's being broadcast live, there and then!'

'So whatever happens, there's nothing they can do about it?' asked Fen.

'Exactly,' said Ricky. 'Now, Stass – can you bring that tape recorder of yours tomorrow? There's bound to be another marching practice after school.'

'Sure,' said Stass. 'What do you want to record?'

'The Mad Ox's marching commands,' said Ricky. 'And now let's use the back way into the pavilion and take a look at the way those loudspeakers are wired up.'

'It's good to see you showing some school spirit at last, and supporting the marching team,' said Mr Farmer, coming up to the gang as they watched the marching practice next day.

Stass clutched his satchel closer to his chest, hoping the teacher wouldn't see the microphone just poking out near the flap. They were standing in front of the pavilion, so that they would be as near as possible to record the loudspeaker commands Mr Maddox was barking out from the pavilion steps.

Ricky said in a whisper, turning away from Stass so that his voice wouldn't be on the tape, 'We enjoy watching the marching, sir.'

'What's wrong with your voice?' asked Mr Farmer.

'Just a bit of a sore throat, sir. Have you seen the birds nesting in that tree, sir?' said Fen, also very quietly.

'You've got a sore throat too, have you?'

'Yes, sir.'

'It must be catching. What birds are you talking about?'

'Over there, sir,' said Fen hoarsely. She wanted to get Mr Farmer away, so that his voice wouldn't be on the tape when they came to play it back. 'I'll show you, shall I, sir?'

Mr Farmer backed away a little. 'No, no, it's all right, I'll look myself. Don't worry. Besides, I don't want to catch your sore throat. I may have to be filmed again teaching in class, and I want to keep my voice, don't I? After all, I am supposed to be one of the stars of the film.'

Mr Farmer moved away from them.

They went on recording the commands, as Mr

163

Maddox roared enthusiastically through the loud-speakers, and the squads marched up and down.

After school, they took the tape machine to the boiler house headquarters, and played it back. The commands came over perfectly.

'It's just as if the Mad Ox was here in the room!' said Edward.

'Now tomorrow,' said Ricky, 'just before the live broadcast, we'll creep in under the pavilion where the wiring is, and wire in our tape recorder so that it plays through one of the loudspeakers. Then, when the Mad Ox is saying his commands through one loudspeaker, we can broadcast our alternative commands through the other. Those marchers will be totally confused.'

'And they won't be able to stop and retake it, because it will be going out live!' said Stass.

'What if they catch us under the pavilion?' asked Edward.

'If they find out what we're up to, I should think the Mad Ox will expel the lot of us,' said Fen.

'It's a risk we'll just have to take,' said Ricky. 'Does everyone agree?'

'YES!' came the immediate reply from the rest of the gang.

The filming of the marching display next day went smoothly enough, after all the rehearsing they had done. Mr Maddox was in roaring form as he shouted out the commands to his team. The Red Spectacles Gang looked on.

'Just look at Kenneth!' said Fen. 'He's so smug you could swear he was a brigadier general.'

'He's swinging his arms so much I wouldn't be surprised if they come off,' said Stass.

'Wait till he hears *our* commands, then we'll see how well he marches!' said Ricky. 'Now, remember, here's the plan. As soon as Harbison's filming finishes, we go casually over to the pavilion, then sneak round behind it and dive underneath into the gap between the floor and the ground. We fix the wires, and wait for the broadcast of the live marching to start. Then we play the tape.'

'I reckon we can get in under the pavilion without being seen,' said Stass.

'Sure,' said Ricky, 'but getting out again may not be so easy!'

'OK, thank you all, that's a wrap for today,' Harold Harbison called to his film crew. He went across to congratulate Mr Maddox. 'Great display, great display!' he said.

'Thank you, thank you!' said Mr Maddox. 'Thank you too, boys and girls!'

The marchers began to move away. Then Mr Maddox shouted: 'Get back in place! It's not over yet, remember. We have to do a repeat performance for the local television show.'

He pointed at the big truck which was standing not far away, between the pavilion and the outdoor swimming pool. On top of the truck a television camera was mounted, and there was another camera further away across the field.

'Our friends from the local station have been lining up their shots as we have been filming for Mr Harbison, so all we need to do is to repeat the march sequence we have already performed so superbly. And on this occasion, you will be seen live and instantaneously, right across the region! Isn't that correct, Miss MacIntyre?'

He turned to a woman in a denim suit, standing near the outside broadcast truck. She gave a thumbs-up sign.

'Very well – there are refreshments for all the marchers in the pavilion here, courtesy of our television friends. Relax and rest, and don't eat too much. I want you all ready and lined up on the field at 5.30, and when I get the cue, I shall issue the first command. Dismiss!'

As his own crew packed up and left for the night, Mr Harbison went across to Miss MacIntyre and said: 'Well, we've got the marching well-organized for you. It will be a cinch for you to put your cameras on to it. Of course, it won't have the finesse of *our* film, naturally . . . '

'We'll manage fine, thank you very much,' said Miss MacIntyre sharply. Harold Harbison smiled and walked away.

13

The marchers crowded towards the pavilion. So did a number of the spectators, hoping they might be able to sneak in and get some free refreshments too. Ricky and the Red Spectacles Gang moved with the crowd, but instead of going up the steps of the pavilion, they went round towards the back. Suddenly they stopped in their tracks as a voice rapped out:

'Where are you off to?'

They turned. The daunting figure of Mrs Froom was standing just behind them. There was a moment of silence. The Red Spectacles Gang stood as still as statues, gazing at the deputy head. Her laser eyes gazed steadily back.

Ricky broke the spell. 'We wanted to watch the marching on TV, in the television room in school,' said Ricky. 'It's such an honour for Spencer's . . . '

'A fat lot you care about the honour for Spencer's!' said Mrs Froom. 'You're just sneaking off early. Get back on to the side of the field with the others, and cheer on the marchers.'

The gang glanced at each other. Ricky said: 'Yes, Mrs Froom.' They all moved back towards the front of the pavilion, while Mrs Froom stood watching them. But instead of staying in front with the rest of the school, Ricky simply led them on round the other side of the pavilion, till they reached the back corner. Ricky put his head cautiously round, in case

Mrs Froom had moved this way. But there was no sign of anyone.

'OK, in we go!' said Ricky. He knelt down and led the way through a gap in the wall, which brought them underneath the pavilion floor. Here it was dusty and damp, and the boards creaked above them as people walked to and fro. The noise of the voices seemed even more deafening down below.

They crept along with their heads kept low – there was less than a metre of space between the ground and the floorboards above their heads. They reached the front wall of the pavilion and crawled along till they came to the steps.

The stairs into the pavilion were wide, and there were gaps between the wooden planks, so that they could see out and get a good view of the marching area.

During their survey, they had been able to trace the cable which led from one of the loudspeakers on the roof, down the wooden pillar and along the back of the steps, to link with the other speaker and the microphone.

It didn't take long for Ricky to connect the loudspeaker to the tape recorder. Now, one of the loudspeakers above was still wired to Mr Maddox's microphone – but the other was linked to the tape recorded by the Red Spectacles Gang.

When the marching began, there would be two lots of commands called out by Mr Maddox, one live, and one recorded – but they would be out of time with each other.

They settled down to wait for the next marching display to begin. Above them the people walking about in the pavilion just over their heads sounded like a herd of buffalo tramping around.

They could hear familiar voices in the general hubbub. Caroline said: 'I have *not* had five sausage rolls already! It was only four.'

Sharon sneezed loudly. Simon said: 'I wish I'd worn my dad's medal.'

'What was it for?' asked Kenneth.

'Distinguished service.'

'What in?'

'Well, in the factory snooker team, actually. But it's still a medal.'

Kenneth said: 'I bet Ricky Redman and his dreadful cronies are green with envy at seeing us being shown on the telly.'

Ricky and the rest smiled at each other. Just then the booming voice of Mr Maddox roared: 'All right, everyone! It's time you assembled on the field! Everybody out! Out you go! And take that sausage roll out of your tunic, Caroline! Outside, all of you!'

The buffalo hoofs thundered above them like a stampede, and they could see the feet clumping down the steps, just a few centimetres away. There was a stumbling clatter as someone tripped and fell, at the bottom of the steps. They could see Sharon sitting on the ground, clutching her ankle. She was only a couple of metres away, but the steps and the darkness underneath them made the gang invisible – or so they thought.

'I've hurt my ankle, sir,' Sharon whimpered, looking up towards the steps where Mr Maddox was standing. Through the gap between the steps, they could see his shoes just in front of their eyes.

'Never mind that now,' said the headmaster.

'Can't you see the programme's about to start? Get out of the way!'

Sharon got up to a kneeling position. She was looking right between the steps. Fen felt as if she was staring straight at her; and her heart missed a beat when Sharon suddenly gave a loud scream.

'BE QUIET!' shouted Mr Maddox.

'It's an animal, sir! I can see its eyes!' wailed Sharon.

'The girl's delirious,' said the headmaster. 'Mr Farmer, kindly remove her at once.'

Mr Farmer came over and helped the whimpering Sharon away from the pavilion.

'Phew, that was close!' Fen whispered.

Over by the TV truck, they saw a lean young man with headphones on say something to the girl in the denim suit. She called across to Mr Maddox:

'Headmaster! We're on the air in one minute from now!'

The marchers were in position, lined up on the field. Stass gripped the recorder, ready to press the PLAY button and start the tape.

The denim girl moved across and stood on the steps beside Mr Maddox. She had smart black boots with chunky heels.

From the gang's viewpoint, it looked as if two pairs of feet had dressed themselves up and were lined up to watch a show.

They could see a man in a tracksuit, wearing trainers, approach to within three metres of the steps. He had a hand-held television camera on his shoulder and was pointing it at Mr Maddox and the girl in the denim suit.

The headphoned man called out: 'Ten seconds!' then 'Nine, eight . . . '

They heard the denim girl say softly: 'Don't be nervous, Mr Maddox, just act naturally.'

Mr Maddox boomed: 'Oh, *I'm* not nervous . . . '

The girl silenced him with an urgent 'SSSSH!' as the headphone man reached 'Four!'

After that, he simply held three fingers up, then two, then one . . . and finally dropped his hand, pointing at the pair on the steps.

The girl said: 'This is Jeannie MacIntyre at Spencer's School, whose superb marching team will be featured in the forthcoming documentary in the series *Schools in the Picture*. Today, we're giving you a preview of the splendid performance viewers will be seeing nationally – and perhaps, who knows, internationally too! Here to mastermind the display is the headmaster of Spencer's School, Mr Max Maddox.'

'Good evening!' boomed the head.

'Well, with that voice,' said Jeannie MacIntyre, with a little laugh, 'it's easy to see how you are able to command this marching team we see here.'

'Oh, yes indeed, yes indeed!' said Mr Maddox. 'Here at Spencer's we believe in discipline, and school spirit, and both of these wonderful qualities are superbly demonstrated in the marching displays for which our school is renowned. In fact, I think I may safely say—'

'Indeed you may, Mr Maddox,' Jeannie interrupted, 'but meanwhile, it's on with the march!'

'Right! Yes! Certainly!' said Mr Maddox, a bit put out at being cut off in midstream. He soon recovered himself, and barked out the command:

'SQUAD . . . atten . . . SHUN!'

The squad came to attention. Mr Maddox shouted:

'SQUAD . . . left . . . TURN!' The squad obeyed. The Red Spectacles Gang peered from their hideout.

Ricky whispered: 'The Mad Ox doesn't seem to realize there's only one loudspeaker working.'

'He's so loud, he hardly needs loudspeakers,' said Fen.

The headmaster was roaring: 'SQUAD . . . by the left, quick . . . MARCH!'

The group stepped off with their left feet, and began marching across the field. Mr Maddox gave the commands to about turn, then to right turn, and the team moved with practised precision. The cameras swivelled and pointed, following their movements.

'OK,' said Ricky softly. 'Alternative Mad Ox, quick . . . PLAY!'

Stass pressed the PLAY button of the recorder, at the part of the tape they'd selected. As the marchers stepped along, they suddenly heard the voice of Mr Maddox from the second loudspeaker, roaring: 'Atten . . . SHUN!'

The marchers looked puzzled. They glanced at one another. One or two of them faltered and stumbled. Ricky and the gang heard Mr Maddox above them say: 'Who said that?'

Unfortunately he still had the microphone close enough for the question to boom out over the loudspeaker. The marchers looked even more bewildered, but they kept on.

Then from the tape loudspeaker came the headmaster's voice again: 'SQUAD . . . by the left, quick . . . MARCH!'

As they were already on the move, the marchers were again puzzled by this command, apparently

172

coming from Mr Maddox himself. They kept on, but many of them were out of step.

'What's happening?' whispered Jeannie MacIntyre.

'I wish to God I knew,' said Mr Maddox, and again his voice carried through the loudspeaker. The marchers looked very startled. The crowd was beginning to snigger.

Mr Maddox roared through the microphone: 'Ignore interruptions! Listen to *me*! SQUAD . . . on the march . . . about . . . TURN!'

The marchers turned, but as soon as they had done so, the taped voice of Mr Maddox roared: 'About . . . TURN!' The squad turned again.

The headmaster snarled in fury: 'About . . . TURN!'

The marchers turned once more. Some of them were looking distinctly giddy. The voice from the tape said: 'Left . . . TURN!'

Mr Maddox called: 'Right . . . TURN!'

'Is it some kind of echo?' asked Jeannie with interest.

'Echo my foot!' yelled Mr Maddox.

The marchers looked wildly towards the pavilion. This was a command they had never heard before.

'SQUAD . . . on the march . . . left . . . TURN!' said the tape.

Mr Maddox said in a thunderous voice of fury: 'SQUAAAAD . . . HALT!'

The marchers thankfully came to a standstill, but just as they did so the taped voice said: 'Right . . . WHEEL!'

Most of the marchers set off again, others stayed where they were. Kenneth was at the head of the ones who set off.

'I said HALT, dammit!' shouted Mr Maddox.

'Now, on the double, change STEP!' said his taped voice.

Some of the marchers stopped, others broke into the running step, as instructed. They bumped into each other. Two or three fell down, and others fell over them.

'It's a *shambles*! It's a bloody *shambles*!' bawled Mr Maddox, and the loudspeaker broadcast his voice all round the playing field, as well as into the homes of several million viewers, who could hardly believe their eyes and ears.

Kenneth decided he would try to retrieve some order from the chaos. He was at the head of a ragged group of a dozen or so marchers who were trying to struggle on.

'Follow me, men!' said Kenneth, in a voice like some gallant commander urging his men to one final assault on the enemy machine-gun post. 'Follow me!'

He marched onwards, with his head turned back to the troop behind him, waving them forward. Because he wasn't looking ahead, he didn't see that he had come to the top of the sloping bank of grass that went down towards the swimming pool. Before he knew it, he had tripped over and was rolling down the bank. The marchers behind just stopped themselves, collapsing in a jumbled heap at the top of the bank.

Kenneth rolled down the bank and tumbled with a splash into the pool.

The voice on the tape said: 'About . . . TURN!'

'SHUT UP!' yelled Mr Maddox.

Then they heard Jeannie MacIntyre say: 'And now from this rather unusual marching display, this is Jeannie MacIntyre at Spencer's School, returning you to the studio.'

'And this is the Red Spectacles Gang, returning from the pavilion,' said Ricky, as Stass disconnected the recorder, and they crawled as quickly as they could to the back of the pavilion to get away from the scene, before Mr Maddox started to investigate.

As they crawled, they heard Jeannie saying to the headmaster: 'Never mind, it will make a wonderful sequence in that programme of great television disasters!'

Mr Maddox gave a loud, long-drawn-out groan, which boomed like a growl of thunder across the playing field.

The gang were just about to crawl out through the gap in the back wall of the pavilion, when Ricky whispered urgently: 'Stop!' They all froze. Just outside, they could hear the voices of Mrs Froom and Mr Farmer.

'It's someone messing about, up on the roof!' rasped Mrs Froom. 'Get a ladder and climb up.'

They could see the legs of the two teachers, through the gap just a few metres away.

'I tell you it was a sound fault – an echo of some kind. A technical hitch!' Mr Farmer was obviously seeking desperately for some solution which didn't involve climbing on to the roof.

'Don't be ridiculous!' said Mrs Froom. 'There's some monkey business here, and I'm going to get to the bottom of it. If you won't fetch a ladder, I will! Where's Grimley?' She strode off towards the school, calling: 'Grimley! Grimley!'

Mr Farmer followed her, saying: 'All right, all right, I'll help, if you insist . . .'

Their voices went away into the distance. Ricky

put his head out through the gap, looked around, then came back in again and said: 'Right! It's now or never. Everybody out!'

They scrambled quickly out through the gap, and started walking fast towards the school, just as Simon and Caroline and some of the other marchers came round the corner of the pavilion. They were followed by a bedraggled Kenneth, dripping wet from his plunge into the pool. Behind them came a great crowd of the spectators, chattering excitedly.

'Here! Where are you lot going?' Simon asked the gang.

'Get a ladder, get a ladder!' said Ricky. 'There's someone on the roof! Mrs Froom saw them. Hurry!'

The Red Spectacles Gang started running towards the school, after Mrs Froom and Mr Farmer. Some of the crowd ran with them, other people stayed behind, pointing at the roof and looking up and talking loudly.

By the time Mr Grimley and the ladder had been found, the gang had split up and were just part of the crowd that milled around Mrs Froom and Mr Farmer, and egged Mr Farmer on as he climbed on to the roof and reported that he could find nothing.

'I couldn't believe my eyes!' said Fen's mother over dinner that evening. 'I turned on the television and what should I see but this absolutely *ridiculous* display by your school, Fenella. And the language! From the headmaster, too!'

'I thought Spencer's was supposed to be expert at marching,' said Fen's father, looking up from the financial page of his evening paper.

'Oh, it is – usually,' said Fen, 'there was some mess-up with the loudspeaker system.'

'I wonder how that happened,' said Fen's mother.

'I haven't a clue,' said Fen, dabbing her mouth with her napkin, to hide her grin.

Stass's family's shop stayed open till eight in the evening, and he was helping at the counter. The people who came in were all joking and laughing about the programme.

'Did you see that boy take a dive into the pool?'

'Did you see that headmaster's face? I thought he was going to explode!'

'I'll say one thing for your school, Stass, they're great entertainers.'

'You should tell that head to start a comedy series.'

Stass laughed with them, wondering what they'd say if they knew the part he himself had secretly played in the entertainment.

Edward's sister said she couldn't wait to go to his school, if that was the sort of thing they did there: it was funnier than any of the comedians. She asked why Edward wasn't in the marching squad himself.

'Oh, I was doing something very important,' said Edward. 'But it was behind the scenes. Sort of controlling it, really.'

'Controlling that shambles!' grunted his father. 'What a cock-up! I always said that school was no good.'

'No, you didn't, it was you that wanted him to go there,' Edward's mother said. 'Good discipline, you said. Well, if that's discipline, I'm Mary, Queen of Scots!'

'Yes, and you know what happened to her – she was beheaded,' said his father.

Edward realized they'd be arguing for some while. He excused himself and went out to the yard to practise his yo-yo.

Ricky's father hadn't seen the programme, but on his way home from work he'd met Mr McArdle, who had told him all about it.

'He must be exaggerating,' Mr Redman said to Ricky. 'It surely couldn't have been as much of a shambles as that.'

'Oh, it was, Dad, it was,' said Ricky enthusiastically.

His father looked at him suspiciously. 'Ricky, you weren't in the squad, were you?' he asked.

'Oh no, Dad,' said Ricky firmly. 'I wasn't in the squad.'

'Thank heavens for that, anyway. I dare say that headmaster of yours will have a few hard words to say tomorrow.'

As they waited in the playground next morning for the signal to go in, the Red Spectacles Gang felt uneasy. Supposing Mrs Froom remembered seeing them behind the pavilion, and decided they were behaving suspiciously? Even then, she couldn't prove anything. But what if they had left some evidence behind, and she thought of looking *under* the pavilion, instead of on the roof?

When Mrs Froom came out on to the steps, they half feared she would come striding across to them with an accusing finger pointed. But she simply blew her shrill referee's whistle as usual, and they all trooped inside to assembly.

Mr Maddox did indeed have a lot of hard words to say. In fact, he came out with all the threats and lamentations he could muster: 'Disgrace to the school. . . . Diabolical mischief-making. . . . Made us a laughing stock. . . . Culprits will be found and punished . . .'

At one point he was interrupted by a very loud sneeze – then another. But this time it wasn't Sharon, it was Kenneth.

'Poor Kenneth,' said Fen. 'He must have caught a chill after that unexpected swim.'

'Stass – what's the matter?' whispered Ricky. 'You look as if you'd seen a ghost.'

'Yes, a real one this time,' said Edward.

'The tape recorder!' Stass said hoarsely. 'It was still in my satchel when I brought it to school this morning. I put the satchel down while I was looking at the notice board in the hallway – and I've just realized I forgot to pick it up.'

'The tape recorder!' said Ricky. 'And the tape that's on it . . . ?'

'Yes,' said Stass miserably. 'It's the one with the Mad Ox's commands!'

After assembly, they pushed their way through the crowds to get into the hallway, and rushed across to the notice board. There was no sign of the satchel. They knocked at Mr Grimley's door and asked him if he'd seen it, but he had been in his room all the time.

During the morning break, they didn't even join the rest of the school, who were being filmed in the playground. They went on searching everywhere they could think of, but the satchel was nowhere to be seen. They didn't want to ask any of the teachers,

179

in case they asked what was in the satchel, and wondered why they seemed quite so worried about it.

As they hunted through the empty classrooms, they could hear Harold Harbison calling out: 'Just act naturally, boys and girls! Play away, play away, just like you normally would.'

Once, Ricky looked out of the window and saw Kenneth being filmed doing an elaborate demonstration with a cricket ball, showing an admiring group how to grip it for an off-break. Then just as he was raising his arm to bowl, he doubled up and gave an enormous sneeze.

The ball flew off at an angle and hit Simon in the chest. Simon started spluttering.

'CUT!' shouted Harold Harbison.

Ricky smiled – but he couldn't really enjoy the scene as he might have done. They still hadn't found the missing satchel which might give them all away.

They hadn't even had time to plan any tricks or disturbances for Miss Grenfell's lesson after the break. It was her turn to be filmed for the television programme.

While the rest of the class chattered excitedly, and the crew tested their equipment, the Red Spectacles Gang sat gloomily racking their brains, trying to think where the satchel might possibly be. Perhaps some boy or girl had pinched it – and if so, they might soon play the tape that was on the recorder and start putting two and two together.

Miss Grenfell came in with a cheery 'Good morning, girls and boys.'

'Good morning, Miss Grenfell.'

The teacher walked up to the front of the classroom. She was wearing a close-fitting outfit in bright red, with an expensive-looking silk scarf round her neck. Her hair looked glossy, and her walk was slinkier than ever before.

Ricky gave a whistle.

Miss Grenfell said: 'Quiet please!' She put the briefcase she was carrying on the desk, and went into a huddle with Harold Harbison, who was talking earnestly and gesturing as he explained how they wanted to film her lesson.

Then she went to the platform and waited for the crew to be ready. When Mr Harbison called: 'Action!' she said: 'Today, I shall be testing you on some of the key dates in English history. For as I always say, if there were no dates, there'd be no history, and then where would we be?'

She gave a tinkling laugh, glancing towards the camera. The class obediently laughed too.

'Now, Caroline, I want you to come up to the blackboard and write down the date of the Battle of Hastings, when William the Conqueror invaded England.'

Caroline stood up and came forward. She kept bumping into desks on her way because she was too busy gazing at the camera instead of looking where she was going.

'Cut!' cried the director. Then he said: 'I think this is going to be too difficult for them, Miss Grenfell. Perhaps you should simply ask them for the dates. And to get some movement into it first, could you perhaps get out some papers and hand them round the class?'

'Very well,' said Miss Grenfell. She opened her briefcase to find some papers. She looked inside, and then looked at Mr Harbison. 'If I could delay just a moment,' she said, 'there's something I forgot.'

Mr Harbison shrugged.

'I found this in the hallway today,' said the teacher. 'I've been asking round my various classes, but I haven't found the owner yet. It contains a tape recorder, among other things.'

Out of the briefcase she pulled the satchel, and held it up for the class to see. Then she took out the recorder and put it on the desk.

'That's mine, miss!' Stass cried, leaping up. He rushed up to the platform eagerly.

'You're sure?' said Miss Grenfell.

'Oh yes, miss.'

'You should all put your names on your satchels and your things,' said the teacher. 'I suppose I should really ask you to prove it's yours, Anastasios . . . '

'Oh, it's mine all right, miss. Really.'

'Yes, it's his, miss,' said Ricky.

Miss Grenfell looked undecided. 'Perhaps you have some of that Greek music you like so much, on the recorder, do you?'

She reached her finger towards the PLAY button.

'No, miss, no!' cried Stass. He put his hand on the recorder, quickly pressed the EJECT button, and took the tape out.

'Why don't you want us to hear it?' asked Miss Grenfell.

With relief, Stass suddenly remembered something. He quickly turned the tape over in his hand, and put it back in the machine.

'Oh, you can hear it if you like, miss!' He smiled and pressed the PLAY button.

Ricky held his breath. Had Stass gone raving mad? he wondered. But Ricky hadn't seen him turn the tape over. So he laughed with relief as the melodious twanging rhythms of a vigorous Greek dance came from the recorder. Ricky stood up and began to clap in time to it. Fen and Edward joined in.

'That will do!' said Miss Grenfell sharply. 'We have some important filming to do.' She patted her hair, and smiled sweetly at Harold Harbison, who was beginning to get impatient. 'You may have your tape recorder back, Anastasios – and your satchel. And take more care of them in future.'

'I will, miss. Thank you, miss!' said Stass, doing a few quick dance steps as he made his way back to his desk.

14

The film crew seemed to be everywhere during the rest of that day. Instead of following their usual custom of filming a scene, then filming it again because of technical problems, then trying it again, and yet again, they started rushing about from one location to the next.

They filmed a staged cricket match, then although it wasn't the right season, they insisted the rugby team do a scrum and line-out immediately afterwards, while the girls played lacrosse on the next pitch. They rushed up to the bell-tower to do some high-angle shots, and clattered down again to take exteriors of the front of the school.

On his way to the last class of the day, Ricky came across the wild-haired sound engineer in the hallway, rummaging among his box of equipment. He saw him pause and take a quiet swig from his flask.

'Keeps out the cold,' the sound man grinned as he saw Ricky watching him. 'Nearly empty,' he said, shaking the flask. 'Still, not to worry. We're wrapping at the end of today, after the evening shots.'

'But what about tomorrow?' asked Ricky urgently. 'Saturday – in the square. Our busking act!'

Don't know anything about that,' said the sound man. 'Anyway, no can do. Industrial action.'

'What? But we've arranged . . .'

'Can't be helped. It's a dispute. The union. Over-time ban, see? That means no weekend working. That's why Hapless Harry is rushing us around so much – to get it all in the can.'

'Jimmy, where are you?' shouted the director, poking his head in at the main door. 'We're filming Mrs Froom on the steps, blowing the whistle.'

'That should bust the recording gear,' said Jimmy pleasantly. 'If the old bat's face hasn't already cracked the camera lens!'

Then he saw Mrs Froom outside, standing just behind the director. 'Coming, boss!' he said hastily, and picked up his equipment.

Ricky hurried away to the art room. Mrs Turner was correcting exam papers at her desk, while the class worked on their own, each doing a drawing of the school crest.

Ricky gathered the gang into a huddle, while they pretended to be talking about their drawings. He explained what he'd just heard from Jimmy the sound engineer.

'What can we do?' whispered Edward.

'We'll just have to do the act today.'

'But where?' asked Fen.

'We'll have to do it in the rubbish yard – it's our only hope. I'll see Hapless Harry after this class and try and persuade him.'

'See who?' asked Stass.

'The director. Mr Harbison. That's what the crew call him.'

'Any more talking, and you'll all be kept in after school,' said the rasping voice of Mrs Turner. The gang quickly broke up and tried to look busy at their own drawings. They couldn't risk being kept

185

in, when they planned to be busking for the cameras.

Ricky and Fen didn't find it easy to persuade Harold Harbison.

'We've been practising so hard,' said Ricky. 'We really want to show how creative the school is.'

'It's so different from other schools,' said Fen.

'Hail, glorious Spencer's!' said Ricky.

'Our school of renown,' said Fen.

'And *your* school too, Mr Harbison,' said Ricky.

'Oh, all right, kids,' said the director. 'For the sake of the old school, what?'

'And it will still be a secret, just to impress Mr Maddox later?'

'Yes, yes, all right. I'll say we're just doing some exteriors round the back, and we'll be doing the final evening shots after that.'

The preparations were frantic. Fen had to go home and fetch Baskerville – much to her mother's surprise. She had her friends in for a bridge afternoon, and was in the middle of some intense bidding when Fen rushed in and picked up the cat from its dozing place on the hearth rug.

'Fen, what are you doing home so early?' her mother asked, as the rest of the ladies looked at her daughter with some disapproval.

'I'm not really home, Mum, I have to fetch Baskerville,' said Fen.

She dashed out of the door, but she heard one of the ladies say in very snooty tones: 'Really, the manners of the young nowadays . . . !'

They hastily changed into their costumes and closed

the door of the boiler house behind them. Whatever happened, they didn't want their secret head-quarters to be discovered.

They admired each other's appearance, and admired Baskerville too. Her lacy collar made her look a bit like the dog in the Punch and Judy show. The cat seemed to sense the excitement: its purr was like a continuous rumble of thunder.

Ricky suddenly had an alarming thought: they had simply got into the yard in their usual way, using the back-scrambling and the stilts. But when the film crew arrived at the gate, they'd find it padlocked.

But just then they heard the voice of Mr Grimley at the gate.

'I don't know why you want to film in here, but at least you'll find it tidy – I keep it neat, I do, now that that blooming dog can't get in. He ought to be put down . . .'

The bolt was pulled back, and the gate swung open. Mr Grimley said: 'I'll leave you to it, then. I've got things to do.'

Looking through the spyhole in the door, Ricky thought he saw Mr Grimley give a thoughtful glance towards the boiler house. Then he went away.

Mr Harbison entered the yard, followed by Fiona, who looked around her loftily, as if filming in a rubbish yard was far from the sort of thing she was used to. They were followed by the rest of the crew.

'Well, that's the limit!' said the director, looking round the yard. 'The little so-and-sos haven't even turned up!'

Then he and the crew stood and gazed in amazement, as the Red Spectacles Gang came bursting out of the boiler house and lined up in a dramatic pose: Ricky at the back with his mortarboard and his black moustache, Edward with his spectacled bird's head on one side, and Stass in his dazzling tracksuit on the other. Fen sat on the cat basket, in front of Ricky, with her banjo at the ready. Baskerville was perched on her shoulder, still purring loudly.

'Well!' said Harold Harbison. 'Your outfits get first prize for originality. A bit of a change from the old school uniform, what?'

The camera and lights were quickly set up, and the sound engineer put his microphones in place. Ricky thought he seemed to be stumbling and staggering a bit. As he worked, he sang tuneless snatches of songs from old stage musicals.

'He ought to be in the act!' grinned Stass.

'Baskerville sings better than he does!' said Fen.

Then Harold Harbison called: 'OK, boys and girls, show us what you can do! We haven't got much time, so we'll go for a take straight away.'

The banjo twanged into action. The gang leapt into lively movement at once. Ricky juggled his oranges and his plate with superb showmanship. Edward flicked his sparkling yo-yo up, down and around. Baskerville's hind-legs walking was so confident it almost looked as if the cat was dancing. Fen played the banjo, her fingers moving with amazing speed, and Stass danced like a whirling, zooming wonder man.

When Ricky climbed on to his stilts, he came forward and began to join Stass in the dance, hopping around like Long John Silver. As the final chords of the banjo signalled the end, Ricky jumped off his stilts and took a flourishing bow, with Stass and Edward beside him, and Fen holding Baskerville triumphantly up in the air.

The sound engineer was applauding, and calling: 'Fantastic! Bloody fantastic!'

The cameraman said: 'Astonishing, what they do in school these days.'

'Isn't it?' said Harold Harbison.

Just then they heard an ear-splitting eruption of yaps, snarls and screeches. Baskerville and Basil, the headmaster's terrier, were circling each other, ready to fight. The film crew must have left the gate ajar, and the dog had seen an unexpected chance to get at his old haunts again.

Fiona was shrieking: 'Stop it! Stop it!' and beating at the dog with her clipboard.

'Grab them before they savage each other!' said Harold Harbison.

'May the best man win!' said the sound engineer.

Baskerville leapt at the dog as she had done before, and landed on its back. She clung on as the terrier rushed madly around the yard, trying to shake the cat off. The dog crashed into a light stand and knocked it over, tangled itself in the microphone cables, bashed its nose on the camera tripod, fell down, got up, and finally admitted defeat and ran out of the yard, yelping.

Baskerville strolled casually across the yard, back to Fen.

As the crew surveyed the chaos, the sound engineer took a swig from his flask and said: 'That is some cat!'

Some days later, at assembly, the headmaster announced that a date had been set for the film

189

about Spencer's to be screened on national television. It coincided with the last day of term, so he had decided to hold a gathering for the parents and the governors and local dignitaries from the town, so that they could all watch the broadcast together.

Without doubt, they would realize then that the tireless work he and his staff had been doing here had made Spencer's School the great pride of the town, and indeed of the nation.

The entire school would be expected to attend, in their best uniforms. The adults would be seated, and the pupils would stand at the sides and at the back of the hall. Giant screens would be placed on the stage so that everyone could have a good view of the programme.

When the day came, the Red Spectacles Gang watched from their corner of the playground while a large green and white marquee was put up just beside the main door. Then a caterers' van came in and parked beside it. People started carrying trestle tables and boxes of bottles and glasses into the tent.

'The Mad Ox is really making a production out of it, isn't he?' said Fen.

'Wait till he sees the production *we've* made on the film!' said Ricky.

'I wonder what old Sir Rumbelow will make of it all,' said Edward, looking at the statue.

'He's probably a bit put out that he hasn't got a starring role,' said Stass.

'At least we should make sure he's noticed,' said Ricky, 'and I've got an idea how we can do it . . . '

The programme was being broadcast at seven

o'clock. At six, the parents and the governors began arriving. They were a little surprised to see that the statue of Sir Rumbelow Spencer was wearing a cowboy hat. A group of them stood round the statue, pointing up at it.

Mr Maddox, wearing a new suit, came out on to the main steps and hurried across to greet his guests.

'You are welcome, you are welcome!' he roared, extending his hand. Then he noticed the upward glances, and looked up himself.

'Good thundering gracious!' he boomed. 'Who did that?'

He glared at the groups of pupils who were gathered in the playground. The Red Spectacles Gang gazed back, looking as puzzled as the rest.

'Those stilts have really got a lot of uses, haven't they?' said Ricky softly.

'That was high-risk stuff,' said Edward nervously. 'Someone might easily have seen us.'

'I knew all the staff would be at home tarting themselves up half an hour before the start,' said Ricky. 'Besides, what's life without a bit of danger?'

Mr Maddox turned towards the school and yelled: 'GRIMLEY!' The caretaker came out of the main door.

'What is it now?' he asked.

'Kindly get that hat off Sir Rumbelow! At once!'

Mr Grimley went back in, muttering, to fetch his ladder. The headmaster turned a beaming smile on the guests, and said:

'Do please come and join us for a glass of wine and a savoury before the show.'

The group of parents and governors moved across

the playground towards the marquee. Some of the teachers emerged from the marquee to greet them.

A black limousine came to a halt in front of the gates. Mrs Froom hurried to the headmaster as he was shepherding the parents and governors across the playground.

'Mr Maddox – the mayor is arriving,' said Mrs Froom.

'The mayor!' boomed Mr Maddox, glancing up at the statue. 'Can't you tell him to drive round the block a couple of times?'

'I beg your pardon?' Mrs Froom's frown was as icy as her smile.

'Oh, never mind, it's too late now,' said Mr Maddox. He hurried forward to greet the Mayor and his party as they got out of the car. At that same moment, behind him, Mr Grimley came out of the school doors with his ladder, and propped it up against the statue of Sir Rumbelow. He looked up at it uncertainly.

Kenneth, who was hovering nearby, hoping he might be introduced to the VIPs, saw a chance to be in the limelight. 'Let me do it, Mr Grimley,' he said.

Before Mr Grimley could reply, Kenneth began climbing the ladder.

As the headmaster shook hands with everyone, and gave a wordy speech of welcome, Kenneth reached the top of the ladder. But he still couldn't quite reach the hat, so he stepped off the ladder on to the flat top of the plinth on which the statue stood.

'Quick!' said Ricky. They moved across to join the group of pupils who had gathered to watch.

'I think it would be easier for him to get down if

we moved the ladder over to the other side,' said Ricky. 'Give me a hand, Stass.'

He winked at Stass. They took the ladder away, but instead of moving it to the other side, they laid it down on the ground.

'Hey, what are you doing?' called Kenneth in alarm.

Just then, Mr Maddox turned and said to the mayor: 'Please come this way, Your Worship . . . '

The mayor stopped and said: 'Good heavens!' They all followed his glance, looking up at the statue. There was Sir Rumbelow in his cowboy hat, with the quivering figure of Kenneth embracing him, as though they were about to set out across the floor in a ballroom dance.

'What a spectacle!' said the mayor's wife.

'What spectacles!' whispered Ricky, touching the rims of his own.

The pupils were allowed crisps and soft drinks from trestle tables set up on the opposite side of the playground to the marquee. Ricky and his friends drifted across to the tent, leaving Simon and Caroline to help Kenneth down from the statue.

The Red Spectacles Gang went round behind the tent and lurked around on the far side of it, between the marquee and the wall of the playground.

There was a din of chatter and the clinking of glasses. Ricky felt along the canvas wall and found a gap where two parts of it joined. He peeped in.

'Give us a sandwich, Dad!' he whispered. His father was startled to see Ricky's head appearing through the tent flap.

'All right,' he said, handing Ricky a smoked

salmon sandwich from the small plate in his hand. 'Should you be here?' he asked.

'Just checking they were treating you all right, Dad,' Ricky grinned, retreating outside.

The four of them took it in turns to peer in through the flap. Fen saw her mother, dressed in a silvery cocktail dress with a bright green jacket, laughing exaggeratedly at something the mayor had said. She happened to glance across and see Fen's head jutting in through the tent flap. She stared. Just as the mayor turned to see what she was looking at, Fen gave a wave and retreated.

Stass spotted his parents too, apparently discussing the quality of the sandwiches and savouries on their plates. They didn't seem to think they were as good as the delicacies they made themselves.

Edward could see his mother talking to Mr Farmer, who was clearly turning on the charm – until Edward's father came across and joined them, and began some kind of argument. Mr Farmer soon excused himself and moved away.

Then they heard Mr Maddox call for silence, and announce: 'Ladies and gentlemen, the hour approaches! In fifteen minutes' time, Spencer's School goes ON THE AIR! So if you would care to move into the assembly hall . . .'

The hall was packed. Ricky and the gang managed to get a place along the side wall, where they could perch on a windowsill. They could get a good view of the giant screens on the stage, and the ranks of blue-uniformed pupils in the back part of the hall and jammed along the aisles, and they could see the colourful rows of adults, the women in their most showy dresses, some with elaborate hats which the people behind them weren't too pleased about.

With five minutes to go, the headmaster brought Harold Harbison on to the stage. He was once more wearing the school blazer which was too small for him, and the school tie.

'This is a proud moment for me,' he began. 'Little did I think, when I was a young boy at this very school, I'm not going to say exactly how many years ago . . . '

Some of the audience laughed dutifully.

' . . . as I say,' went on the director, 'little did I think it would be my proud role . . . '

Mr Maddox was anxiously looking at his watch. He wanted to be able to give his own introductory speech before the programme began. Finally he had only thirty seconds to give a rapid welcome to everyone, which ended with the words:

'Hail, glorious Spencer's – and on with the show!'

He was just in time. The screens, which had been showing the station announcer and some trails for other programmes, showed the station symbol. The announcer's voice said:

'And today our series *Schools in the Picture*, visits Spencer's School . . . '

There was some applause. The introductory captions went up on the screen, with music behind. Then there was a shot of the face of Sir Rumbelow Spencer on the statue.

'Where's his hat?' Fen whispered.

The voice-over said: 'Sir Rumbelow Spencer, founder of the school that bears his name – Spencer's School, a place with its own individual style of education.'

On to the screen came the face of Mrs Froom,

blowing her whistle shrilly. Then there were shots of the pupils lining up and moving across the playground, into the school. There were excited murmurs of: 'There I am, in the middle!' 'I think that's me!' and some ooohs and aaahs from the parents as they spotted their children. Then the film cut to the marching sequence, and the voice said:

'Discipline is the keynote, here at Spencer's, and precision marching is one of the school's greatest achievements. Keep in step, that's the motto.'

'Except when they're falling about all over the place,' said the gruff voice of a parent. There was some chuckling as people remembered the disastrous live television broadcast.

In the front row, Mr Maddox turned and gave a thunderous glare. If he had been able to spot which parent had spoken, he would probably have given him two hundred lines' punishment on the spot.

Mr Maddox appeared on the screen, walking in the grounds of the school. There was a murmur among the audience.

'The Mad Ox!' said Ricky. He hadn't meant it to be quite as loud as it sounded. Some of the parents chuckled again.

Then they saw Mr Maddox in close-up, looking stern and bristly, booming away about *school spirit* and *discipline* and *the noble tradition of Spencer's*.

As he spoke, there were shots of the school, and the pupils, and games, and more marching, and some of the lessons, including Mr Farmer's.

Instead of using Mr Farmer's voice, they simply showed him addressing the class and drawing on the board. The blazer he had borrowed from Harold Harbison looked even tighter and more absurd on the screen than it had done in real life.

'Look at the Smarmer!' whispered Stass.

'He'll never make a TV star!' said Edward.

'No, I don't mean on the screen, look at him down there in the front row.'

They looked. Mr Farmer was sitting slumped down in his seat, with his arms folded. He was clearly far from pleased with his appearance in the film. He looked even less pleased when Miss Grenfell leant across and tapped his arm, then pointed at the screen.

Her own face was now there on the television, smiling and talking about King Charles. In the audience, Miss Grenfell turned and beamed radiantly at the parents in the rows behind, as if to say: 'Look – that's *me*!'

The film cut from Miss Grenfell back to Mr Maddox again, much to Miss Grenfell's obvious annoyance. This time the head was waffling on about the need for the old values to be kept up, and the way these were expressed in traditions like the school song.

The Red Spectacles Gang nudged each other, as the sound-track swelled with the voices:

> 'Hail, glorious Spencer's, our school of renown . . .'

The camera travelled slowly along the rows of faces in the hall. Suddenly there was a muttering in the audience, and some giggling. There on the screen were the faces of Ricky, Fen, Stass and Edward, all wearing their red spectacles.

Mr Maddox stood up and moved towards the stage, glaring at the screen. Voices cried: 'Sit down!' He turned and stared around the audience, looking for the four spectacle-wearers, but didn't spot them on their windowsill.

The film had cut to a longer shot of the audience, and in this one the gang could be seen clearly enough among the crowd – but their spectacles had mysteriously disappeared. They could see Mr Maddox rubbing his eyes.

On the film, the singing went on. Ricky and his friends waited eagerly for the third verse. But just after the second one, the music faded down and disappeared, and there was an interview with one of the governors, the mayor's wife. She was a tall, bony woman with a jutting chin and well-groomed grey hair. In the film she was wearing exactly what she was wearing now, in the audience: a black-and-white-check suit, with a very frilly blouse, and a large metallic brooch at her neck.

'We want no sloppy do-as-you-please liberal ideas at Spencer's,' she was saying in the film, 'we want our children to be brought up to conform, to find their due place in society, some to lead, some to obey – but all to serve!'

There was applause from quite a number of the parents, and the mayor's was especially loud. Ricky suspected that if it hadn't been, he'd have got a telling-off from his wife later. It was her turn now to turn and smile at the audience from her front-row seat. But she did more. She actually stood up and took a bow.

Mr Maddox looked put out that she was stealing the limelight, but he soon cheered up as once again his own face appeared on the screen. This time he was on the platform at assembly, gazing down on the school as it sang the school song. And this time, the film was showing the last part of that sequence, when most of the school were mumbling and muttering as they tried to get through the little-known third verse.

But they weren't all mumbling. Clear and high and sweet, the voice of Fen could be heard close to the mike, singing:

'Hail glorious Maddox, our heavenly head –
He feeds us on haddocks and slices of bread.
Though others may think him a funny old fool,
We love Mr Maddox, the head of our school!'

There were puzzled murmurs among the audience, and some chuckles, and some barks of annoyance. They could see the headmaster in the front row, having a furious whispered argument with Harold Harbison, who was gesturing for him to calm down.

Suddenly Mr Maddox stopped arguing and turned to gape at the screen, his mouth open in disbelief. The voice on the sound track was saying:

'But all work and no play makes Jack a dull boy – and here at Spencer's the boys – and the girls – are encouraged to play creatively.'

The Red Spectacles Gang grinned and nudged each other with excitement. There they were, juggling, banjo-playing, dancing, yo-yo-ing, and stilt-walking, while Baskerville did her tricks. Suddenly Mr Farmer stood up and pointed at the screen, shouting: 'That's my mortarboard!'

Mr Maddox stood up as well. He turned to Harold Harbison, and grasping the lapels of his blazer, hauled him to his feet. He put his face close to the startled director's, and snarled: 'What do you mean by it? You've betrayed us! Betrayed your old school!'

'It's creativity! Manual dexterity!' moaned Harold Harbison, as Fiona tried to pull the headmaster away.

The credit titles began to roll up on the screen, as the busking continued. A few of the audience were applauding, others were saying: 'Outrageous!' 'Absurd!' and 'Shouldn't be allowed!'

There was no doubt what the governors thought. The mayor's wife had gathered them round her in a flock, of which she was certainly the boss. She drew herself up to her full height, even towering over Mr Maddox, and said in a voice that cut through the babble:

'Mr Maddox, I shall be calling a governors' meeting about this. I think you have a lot of explaining to do!'

She began to move majestically towards the door of the hall, followed by the scurrying mayor and the group of governors.

As the parents surrounded Mr Maddox, demanding an explanation, Mr Maddox boomed: 'And I know some pupils who have got some explaining to do! Where are those devils?'

Just then, Mrs Froom came to the door of the hall, blocking the governors' exit, and called excitedly: 'Mr Maddox! Mr Maddox! There's a telephone call for you!'

The headmaster growled: 'More complaints, I'm sure. I can't possibly take it now, Mrs Froom . . .'

'Oh, but you must, Mr Maddox,' said Mrs Froom. 'It's not a complaint. It's a lady who runs a children's charity. She's seen the programme and she's staging a big show with a cast of children, and she wants the four that were doing that act at the end of the film to be in it.'

'What?' said Mr Maddox. 'That pack of delinquents?'

Mrs Froom went on: 'She said there was going to be a top member of the royal family at the show, and it would be a great honour for the school.'

The headmaster's expression changed. He gave a thin smile and said: 'I see. Royal, you say?'

'Yes.'

At the mention of royalty, the mayor's wife and the governors immediately changed their attitude. They started chattering to each other in excitement. Ricky, hovering nearby, could hear the word 'royal' being used frequently.

Mr Maddox smiled at the group of governors and said pompously: 'The honour of Spencer's School has always been my first and foremost aim in life. I shall take the call.'

With his head held high, he marched towards the door. Just as he reached it, his eyes met Ricky's. There was a ferocious and menacing glare in the headmaster's eyes, but Ricky gazed back calmly. Mr Maddox swept on, out of the door.

The Red Spectacles Gang decided it was time to fade away, out of the limelight, for the moment. As they moved across the playground, they chanted:

'Stamp your feet, nod your head,
Spectacles on, and we all see red!'

Then Ricky shouted: 'Broadway, here we come!'

As they were passing the statue of Sir Rumbelow Spencer, Edward produced his crumpled-up bird mask from his coat. With a gesture of sheer delight, he flung it up towards the statue. It was a chance in a million, but it worked: the mask landed on the head of the statue.

They all cheered as they hurried out of the playground, just as the parents and governors came trooping out of the school, to find Sir Rumbelow Spencer gazing down on them from his plinth, over a bird's beak, and through round, red spectacles.